2 MINUTES TO MIDNIGHT

MIDNIGHT TRILOGY BOOK 2

L.M. HATCHELL

For my Mam, who gave me my love of books

Phoenix shoved her way through the sea of bodies between her and the demon. "I thought you said this one would be easy?" she groused, attempting to keep sight of Ethan as he was swallowed into the crowd.

If he answered, his response was lost in the drone of conversation that surrounded them. The humans waiting impatiently at the Jervis Street Luas stop were oblivious that the delayed tram was the least of their problems, and she almost envied them. The mindless chatter about the weather and slurred requests to "spare some change" all seemed so *normal*.

As the rain pelted down relentlessly and she was forced to dodge the lethal corner of yet another carelessly wielded umbrella, she wondered where exactly her life had gone so wrong.

Ahead of her, Ethan appeared once more from the black hole of rush hour madness. She fixed her gaze on the werewolf's broad shoulders and ploughed on.

A jangling bell announced an approaching tram and

the horde suddenly surged forward. She dug her heels in as everyone jostled around her for prime position on the moving sardine tin that was pulling to a stop.

"Phoenix!"

Ethan's yell came from the furthest carriage where a flash of yellow slipped through the doors of the tram.

Dammit!

She moved forward with renewed vigour, murmuring vague apologies as she went. Angry shoves and not so pleasant words were the only thanks she got for trying to save the passengers from their own ignorance, but still she pressed on.

Her eyes fell on the frail old man in the bright yellow rain jacket, clutching tightly to a handrail in the furthest carriage. The tram's warning bell sounded once more. Time was up.

Glowing red eyes met her own, and a wide smile split the man's wrinkled face into a grimace of satisfaction as the doors began to close.

Ahead of her, Ethan moved in a blur, disappearing into the packed tram carriage after their target. She cursed under her breath and made a last-minute dive for the doors nearest her. She pulled herself clear just as they snapped closed.

The smell of stale sweat was the first thing that hit her, assaulting her heightened senses as it carried on a wave of recirculating heat. She cursed the vampire side of her genetics that left her open for such torture.

With a laboured jolt, the Luas began its sluggish shuffle forward. Phoenix shifted position to see past the bobbing heads and found Ethan at the next set of doors. He gave her a grim nod and turned his menacing stare back to the frail old man standing a couple of feet from him.

Only it wasn't a frail old man. Or at least it wouldn't be for much longer if given a choice. Because the demon was on the hunt for a new host. A stronger host. And they couldn't let that happen.

The rattling of the Luas over the tracks became an audible soundtrack to the tension as they picked up speed. Ethan stared at the demon. The demon stared at her. She stared back at the demon. Waiting.

The commuters swayed with the motion of the tram, and every split-second that they blocked her view made the adrenaline in her veins surge. There was a veritable smorgasbord of casualties between her and the demon, and her skin itched with the need to act.

Reaching into the pocket of her leather jacket, she gripped the small amulet Lily had given her earlier that evening. She rubbed her thumb over the smooth stone at its centre.

Would it work?

The young witch had been working day and night on a spell that would allow them to trap a demon, but it was still all trial and far too much error for Phoenix's liking.

Once more the tram began to slow, and she tensed in anticipation.

The intercom announced the next stop. "Four Courts, Na Ceithre Cúirteanna." With a whoosh, the doors opened and the blast of cold air was a sharp contrast to the unnatural heat encasing them.

The demon moved faster than the frail body should have allowed, diving for the open doorway. Shouts of surprise followed in its wake, quickly turning to angry yells as Ethan set off in pursuit, shoving unwitting bystanders to the side to get past.

I guess that's my cue to go. Phoenix leapt to the footpath and raced after them, grateful for the fresh air that filled her lungs.

Irate passengers gawked as she passed, and she gritted her teeth against the effort of restraining her speed. Only when she hit the thick shadows afforded by the stone buildings did she let go of her control.

They needed to stop the demon before it reached the River Liffey. She was still trying to get over the nightmares from her last demon encounter there; she'd be damned if she was letting history repeat itself.

A low growl pulled her up short at a narrow side street. Ethan's familiar signature called to her from the darkness, and her breath hitched. Careful to keep her back tight to the wall, she edged around the corner.

Ethan had the old man cornered at what appeared to be a dead end. Even from a distance, the demon's energy crawled over her skin like a wave of insects. She shuddered and fought the urge to claw at her arms.

The demon's red eyes flickered like flames in the dim light, and foam dripped from the corner of its mouth. It stood tall and defiant, forcing the aged body into a position it probably hadn't seen for many years. Arthritic hands were held in claws that looked as deadly as any blade she'd ever faced, and the gap-toothed smile was a thing of nightmares.

"Have you got it?" Ethan asked, his voice deeper than normal as he allowed his wolf to play close to the surface.

Phoenix nodded, her eyes fixed on the demon as she held up the small amulet still clasped in her hand.

At the sight of the smoky black stone, the demon hissed; it was an unnatural sound that should never have come from a human mouth, let alone the old man before her.

"Do you think it'll work?" Lily's confidence had seemed shaky at best, and last anyone had filled her in, there was no plan B here.

Ethan gave her a wry smile. "Only one way to find out."

Without warning, he launched himself at the demon.

The sudden movement took Phoenix by surprise and she fumbled with the amulet, almost dropping it before she managed to regain her composure.

Grunts of pain and screeches of fury filled the small space, and she tried in vain to block it out. *Concentrate,* she ordered herself, forcing her breathing to slow.

Daily practice meant she could now access her fae power and call on the sun with ease, but her control was still tenuous at best. If she didn't focus, the results could be … unpredictable.

Heat pulled from the centre of her chest and flowed down through her arms, warming the amulet that was cupped in her hands. The words that came from her mouth made no sense to her and felt completely foreign to her tongue, but she repeated them as Lily had instructed.

A glaring white light burst from her palms, blinding her before she had a chance to close her eyes. For a moment, the light was all there was.

In a flash it was gone, and Phoenix found herself unceremoniously dumped on her arse on the cold, wet concrete.

The distant sound of tyres sloshing over the rain-slick roads filled her ears and she looked around in surprise.

Not far from her, Ethan lay slumped against the side of the building with the old man in a heap at his feet. Her hand was empty, and she scrambled to her knees in a panic. Frantically, she searched the ground for the smoky black stone.

Only, it was no longer black.

Midway between her and the demon, what she could only assume was the amulet rested on the pavement. No longer dormant, it now pulsed with life, glowing a fiery red that was eerily similar to the demon's eyes.

She plucked it from the ground and quickly shoved it into her pocket, half expecting it to burn her.

A deep, rumbling groan came from Ethan's slumped form, and he raised his head to cast a wary eye towards the old man lying at his feet.

"Did it work?"

2

Everything ached and Phoenix was beyond weary as she shoved open the heavy wooden door to the pub she called home. Long past closing, darkness filled the space with a calm sense of waiting; the jukebox sat silently in the corner, beer mats rested on the wooden tables, and the taps glistened along the length of the bar. She sighed.

The pub had been her sanctuary ever since she left Darius's vampire lair four years earlier. She'd passed by just as the jukebox was playing her mother's favourite song, and something about the darkness of the place had called to her, pulling her in.

The friendship and acceptance she'd found within these walls were beyond her wildest dreams, and she wanted nothing more than to lock the door behind her and leave the world outside to fend for itself.

"You're back. I was getting worried."

With a tired smile, she turned towards the bar where Abi stood. A fluffy purple dressing gown encased her friend's petite frame, and her long brown hair was tied in a messy bun on top of her head. Worry lines creased Abi's forehead and guilt gnawed at Phoenix.

Humans weren't meant to know about her world; it was one of the primary edicts of the Lore. Abi had taken it all in her stride, but Phoenix could see the knowledge was taking its toll. Darius might have been the one to expose Abi to the Lore, but it was Phoenix who kept her there.

"Sorry for leaving you to close up again." She waved a hand towards the bar, her chest tightening as she tried to remember the last night she'd spent behind it, laughing and joking with customers.

With a dramatic huff, Abi grabbed two bottles of water from the fridge beside her. "What can I say? It's hard to get good staff these days."

Phoenix laughed and a little of the tension eased from her shoulders. She jumped up on one of the wooden bar stools and gratefully accepted the bottle Abi held out to her.

"Did it work?" Her friend's blue eyes were filled with concern, but there was a spark of curiosity in their depths.

Ever since Darius had given her a crash course on all things supernatural – in the form of kidnapping and torture – Abi had demanded to be kept up to date with everything related to the prophecy. Having learned the hard way that lying to her friend was a bad idea, Phoenix had kept her promise to provide Abi with updates, even though she expected Abi to run screaming for the hills any day now.

"I think so. I hope so." She scrubbed a hand over her face. "The man was old. I'm not sure if he'll make it. We managed to trap the demon in the amulet, but the possession takes its toll."

"You're finding more and more demons lately. It's not a good sign, is it?"

Phoenix let the silence speak for itself.

It had been a little over a month since Ethan had arrived at her door and she'd learned of the prophecy that would end humanity – the one she was supposedly the cause of. In those few weeks she'd been attacked more times than she could count, found her long-lost parents, been betrayed by the man she'd thought of as family, and lost her parents all over again. You'd really think she was due for a break.

Fate seemed to disagree.

No one wanted to say it, but they all knew what was happening. More demons meant only one thing: the fabric was weakening. Her parents' sacrifice had been enough to stop Darius's spell and close the tear he'd created, but it was becoming very apparent that it hadn't been enough to stop the prophecy. Their sacrifice had been pointless.

The thought brought with it a throbbing ache in her chest that matched the one forming between her eyes. She took a long swig of water and hopped down from the bar stool.

"Phoenix ..." Abi bit her lip, hesitating.

She gave her friend what she hoped was a reassuring smile. "I'm going to try get some sleep. Take the night off tomorrow. I'll cover the bar to make up for being such a lousy employee."

"I might need more than one night off to make up for that."

She swatted Abi playfully and let her friend's laughter wrap around her like a comfort blanket as she headed upstairs to the apartment they shared. Not bothering to put on any lights, she made a beeline for her bedroom, closed the door, and flopped onto her bed fully clothed.

The cool, fresh sheets did little to ease the pain in her skull. The pillow over her face didn't work either. She sat up with a huff, leaned back against the headboard, and hugged the pillow to her chest.

Why wouldn't her head just shut up? Every night after patrolling it was the same. Memories and what-ifs consumed her thoughts, growing louder and more insistent the moment she closed her eyes. The ever-looming threat of the prophecy and the distinct feeling they were doing little more than fire-fighting was exhausting.

The close proximity to Ethan didn't help either. Especially not when he was making such an obvious effort to avoid any kind of physical contact with her. It wasn't that she cared or anything, but he'd kissed her, not the other way around.

And still, all of that felt irrelevant.

She reached her hand towards the small wooden box that rested on her bedside locker. Her fingers traced the rough etchings of the sun emblem that represented her mother's fae lineage, and she let the lingering scent of herbs wash over her. The ache in her chest turned into a crushing pain that made it difficult to breathe.

It had been almost a week since Ethan had helped her prepare the Ritual of Passing for them, two weeks since they'd sacrificed themselves to save her. She still couldn't bring herself to put the box away. If she did, she'd have to admit the truth.

They were gone.

Ten years. Ten long years she'd spent wondering if they were alive or dead, and never once had she felt their loss as acutely as she did now. When they stepped into that void, they took with them any possibility of denial.

All she was left with now was the crushing fear that the Ritual hadn't been enough, that their souls were trapped forever.

Ethan peeled his eyes open with effort. Sunlight streamed in through the bedroom window and he squinted, trying to untangle his thoughts from their stupor. Vague fragments of a dream clung to him: green eyes, red hair, a kiss that lit his whole body on fire.

What time is it?

He shook his head in a vain attempt to clear the fog. Late night patrols were taking a toll on his body clock, and it took a minute for the vibration of his phone to register through the grogginess. He bolted upright in the bed.

Adrenaline chased away the last of the sleep fog as he rummaged in the tangled sheets to find his phone. The name on the screen only calmed his heart rate marginally.

"Dad."

"I've been waiting on you to call." Cormac's deep voice held an edge of irritation, but Ethan was more than used to his Alpha being frustrated with him.

"I know. I was hoping she'd have changed her mind by

now, but the bloody woman just won't see sense. So long as Abi is here, she refuses to leave."

He ground his teeth in frustration. It had been two weeks since they'd contacted the Council Liaison Office stupidly looking for the Council's assistance. Two whole weeks during which the Council had no doubt been notified of the existence of a hybrid and were making plans to act. Not to mention the fact that Darius was still out there somewhere. They were working on borrowed time, and every second Phoenix insisted on being stubborn just put her in more danger. But would she listen?

"It's not safe for her, Ethan. Or for the human."

"Don't you think I know that?" He tugged a hand through his unkempt hair. "I'd like to see you convince her."

Cormac's hearty laugh boomed down the phone. "She sounds like your mother."

The thought of his stubborn, strong-willed mother brought a smile to Ethan's face, and after a moment, he found himself laughing too.

"There's something else you should know." Cormac grew serious. "I contacted William. I was due to check in with him anyway, so I thought I could feel him out a bit. The Council have called an emergency assembly tomorrow night."

Ethan's blood ran cold. William was his father's cousin and sat on the Council as head of the werewolves. If he'd been called to an emergency meeting, it could only mean one thing.

"Did you tell him about Phoenix?"

"What do you think I am, a young pup?"

"Sorry, it's just ..." He trailed off before he could put his fear into words and give it life.

The meeting couldn't mean anything good for Phoenix. It was true that she hadn't technically broken any of the Council's edicts – she could hardly be blamed for being born a product of an inter-species relationship. But with her parents now dead, the Council would need someone to make an example of, and what better person than the hybrid who was also responsible for triggering a doomsday prophecy.

"She's still welcome here." Cormac's soft-spoken words broke through his thoughts. "All of your friends are welcome here. Come home, Son."

And with that, he was gone.

Darius stepped out of the portal and into the large amphitheatre at the centre of the Council headquarters in Brussels. He pulled his black cloak low over his head and kept his face angled so that no one would see the burns that still marred the left side of his face. His right hand clenched a silver as scanned the room, the searing pain focusing his mind as he prepared for what was to come.

Around him, the chamber began to fill as other Witnesses stepped through similar portals and formed a sea of identical black robes. The supernatural signatures were so potent that they mixed together to form something almost unrecognisable, but all were accounted for: vampire, werewolf, fae, witch, and shifter.

All pure blood. As it should be.

He weaved between the stone pillars, keeping to the shadows as he made his way closer to the platform at the front of the room. The low hum of conversation surrounded him, but he ignored the other Witnesses. They were irrelevant.

Once the last portal closed and they were closed in by solid stone walls, a hollow gong rang out. A hush fell over the room and the lights dimmed.

All eyes turned towards the raised platform where five figures now stood. Shrouded in blood red cloaks, their faces were hidden and their forms indistinct. Power emanated from the group and the air grew heavy with its oppressive weight.

The Council.

Anger flared in Darius's chest and he clenched his teeth against their not-so-subtle show of superiority. They knew nothing of power, but they would soon enough.

Like sheep, the Witnesses took their places, forming a semicircle around the platform. Another gong rang out, and a man stepped forward through a break in the crowd. His fitted grey suit immediately set him apart from those surrounding him, and Darius sneered.

Vicktor. He knew the snivelling weasel wouldn't be able to hold his nerve.

As he watched, the chief representative of the Council Liaison Office bowed his head in reverence to the five figures before him. One by one, the Council lowered their hoods.

First, the long red hair and sultry pout of Méabh, the head of the fae, became visible. Darius couldn't help but note the resemblance to Jessica Rabbit – if Jessica Rabbit had magic powers and was inclined to slit your throat.

Next, William's rugged features were revealed as he shoved the hood back from his face. The head of the werewolves had a wild, unkempt appearance that matched the feral quality of his signature. He seemed completely out of place in such an official setting, yet he held himself with an assurance that left no question as to his position.

Diana, the head of the witches, followed suit. Her long blonde hair appeared almost like a halo that was starkly contrasted by her resting bitch face. Kam, the head of the shifters, who was easily identifiable by his shorter stature, stood beside her. He, too, lowered his hood, revealing Asian features and an unreadable expression.

Vlad, the head of the vampires, was the last to remove his hood. More like a politician than the head of a powerful supernatural species, he graced the room with his smarmy smile.

Darius gripped the coin tighter in his hand as he pushed down the urge to wipe the smile away in a slow and excruciating manner. This vampire wasn't fit to stand where his Sire had. It was an insult to Il Maestro's legacy and their entire species that they were now forced to bow down to *this*.

Patience, he reminded himself as the silver seared into his palm.

In a gesture filled with all the arrogance of the man, Vlad stepped forward, taking centre stage. "You may speak," he ordered, his voice ringing clear throughout the chamber.

"Council." Vicktor cleared his throat and straightened his suit jacket. "Witnesses. It is with a grave heart that I stand before you today. The CLO was recently contacted by a member of our society. A werewolf. He expressed some concerns regarding recent activity in the Lore and wanted to speak to the Council. Of course, we don't normally entertain such requests, but this werewolf had knowledge of a certain prophecy ...”

Murmurs filled the chamber, creating an anxious hum. Darius tensed. Just how much did Vicktor intend to divulge?

“... And he claimed to be in the presence of a hybrid.”

Silence.

For what felt like an eternity, no one spoke. The implication of Vicktor's statement settled around the room, acting like a weight that pinned everyone in place.

“So, Cassandra saw true,” Diana whispered, her words and the resignation they held clearly audible in the deafening silence.

At the mention of the Seer's name, chaos broke out around Darius. Angry exclamations and worried cries that achieved nothing. The prophecy was infamous among those privy to the Council's history; it was a closely guarded secret that many centuries ago foretold the coming of the Horsemen ... and an end to their way of life.

Fools, all of them. They clung to their way of life like it was something of worth, like they'd all forgotten the true greatness of the Lore. They settled for scraps and fought against the inevitable. Not Darius.

While they cowered in fear of the rising tide, he welcomed it. And for that, he would be rewarded. They would see the folly of their ways when he finally took his place at the right hand of the Horsemen. *They* would bow to *him*.

“How do we know it's true?” a voice called from the crowd.

Murmurs of agreement and similar questions followed,

the room only falling quiet when Vlad held up a hand to silence them.

"Did this werewolf provide any proof of his claim?" William crossed his arms in front of his chest and raised an eyebrow in undisguised scepticism.

There was something oddly familiar in his expression, but Darius didn't have time to think on it as Vicktor nodded in response to the question and the room once more erupted around him.

"SILENCE." Vlad motioned for Vicktor to continue, a single warning glance enough to bring order.

"The werewolf spoke the truth. There is a hybrid," Vicktor confirmed solemnly. "I met with them both personally ... to discuss their concerns."

"It would appear our attempts to stop the prophecy have failed." Méabh sashayed forward, stopping just ahead of Vlad. She flipped her hair over her shoulder and gave him a saccharine smile. "Your edict doesn't seem to have had the effect you hoped for."

The vampire snarled.

"Enough." Kam didn't move from his position or raise his voice. If anything, the Japanese shifter appeared almost bored with the proceedings. Looks could be very deceiving however, and both Vlad and Méabh retreated back into line at his order. "The prophecy has been triggered. We must decide our next steps."

Each of the Council members pulled up the hood of their cloak, and the lights of the chamber dimmed while they deliberated among themselves.

Darius turned his gaze to Vicktor while he waited. The CLO rep stood stiff, his hands clasped in front of him as he pointedly kept his eyes forward. All it would take was one wrong word on his part and Darius's plans would be made significantly more difficult. Perhaps the weasel had outlived his usefulness.

Only a couple of minutes passed before the room brightened, and the Council turned back to face the Witnesses with their hoods lowered. There was a tension between them that indicated not all were happy about the decision they'd arrived at.

Once more, it was Vlad who stepped forward. "For the sake of all the Lore, the hybrid must die."

The night air was crisp as Darius slipped unseen from the Council chambers. He'd heard all he needed to hear, and the fraught discussions and concerned murmurings were of little consequence to him.

A block away from the Council building, he found Vicktor waiting for him in a narrow alley that stank of garbage and other unfavourable aromas that burned the back of his throat. The CLO rep squirmed and tugged the collar of his tailored coat close as he made a concerted effort not to touch anything in the dingy space.

"I was hoping to speak to you." Vicktor gave an impatient huff as his body twitched with its obvious desire to escape the alley.

Darius inclined his head and stepped into the shadows, effectively blocking the other man in.

"I assume you heard the decree?"

"Yes. And I'm not pleased, Vicktor. We need the hybrid

alive. I warned you not to approach the Council with this information."

The CLO rep squared his shoulders, his defiance and snooty air bringing him closer to a final death than he could have possibly imagined.

"You've been missing for two weeks, Darius. I couldn't wait any longer. Your name has been kept out of it for now, and I've convinced them to let the CLO organise the hit. That is already more than I'm comfortable doing."

Darius's hand flexed involuntarily, and he put it into his pocket to stop himself from tearing out the man's throat.

"Comfort is not something we have the luxury of if we're to restore the Lore to its former glory. You know that." Darius kept his tone amicable despite the murderous thoughts playing through his mind. There'd be time for that when he got what he needed. "If the Council succeeds, we'll be back to square one. All of our work will have been for nothing."

Vicktor picked his briefcase up off the ground and brushed it off with a grimace. "If your hybrid is as impressive as you say, she will be able to fend for herself. If not? Well then ..."

With that, he pushed past Darius and stalked from the alley.

4

Lily tossed and turned in the bed. Sweat-soaked sheets tangled around her legs and she kicked at them, biting back a scream of frustration. Her eyes burned with exhaustion and she longed for a single night of dreamless sleep, but every time she closed her eyes, the thoughts came.

Darkness had become a familiar companion since Annabelle's death. Night after night she lay in her sister's bed, clutching the stuffed unicorn that had been Annabelle's since she was a baby. If she tried hard enough, she could still catch a hint of her sister's scent from the soft toy and unwashed sheets. When she closed her eyes, she could still picture her sister's innocent smile. But it was all fading. She was running out of time.

That thought brought with it a panic greater than any of the other memories or what-ifs that plagued her. The thought that her sister would fade from memory before she could do anything to stop it.

She flung the covers off her legs and sat up in the bed,

panting as her chest grew tighter. Her fists clenched and unclenched reflexively. It was as if all the oxygen had been sucked from the room. She forced herself to close her eyes and count to twenty.

You're not going to die, she reminded herself. *You wouldn't be that lucky.*

After a time, her breathing slowed and her lungs once more obeyed the command to expand. Resigned to yet another sleepless night, she slipped from the bed and checked the bedroom door to make sure it was locked.

Ethan and the others had turned in hours before, but she paused for a second, listening for any sign of movement in the apartment.

Only when she was satisfied did she return to the bed. She reached her hand under the mattress and pulled out a box roughly the size of a book. Wooden, and covered in paint that wasn't quite white anymore, there were scuff marks along the edges and the glass top was smudged with fingerprints. Four faces smiled back at her from the photo held within that glass, and her fingertips shook as she tenderly traced the image of her family.

Two minutes. That was all the time she would allow herself. If she looked at the picture any longer, she would break.

With a shuddering breath, she opened the metal clasp and raised the lid. Even in the darkness, the Ouroboros gleamed. Preparing herself for the guilt that always came with her first touch, she lifted the gold plaque out of the box and held the weight in her hands.

Memories came flooding back unbidden: standing in

the dark underground chamber, the walls painted with blood and the aftereffects of death. The lingering taint of black magic. The realisation that it wasn't over.

When the fabric began to tear and they discovered exactly what Darius had achieved with his spell, she'd almost been relieved. They'd failed. They didn't have to fight anymore. Soon, it would be over and she could be with Annabelle and her parents again. The aching emptiness would be gone.

It was only when someone mentioned the Ouroboros that a new possibility occurred to her. She could fix it all. Annabelle's death, Darius's spell, all of it. She could turn back time and make it as if it never happened.

But in order for her to do that, she would need the Ouroboros. Which meant no one else could have it.

On the rare nights when sleep came, Lily found herself back in that chamber, watching Phoenix's world shatter as her parents stepped into the black void. The weight of the Ouroboros would grow heavy in her hands as she silently let Marcus and Aria sacrifice themselves. It would pull her down and she'd find herself drowning in a sea of red. Only then would she wake up, gasping for breath with tears streaming down her cheeks.

What was worse than any of that, however, was the look on Aria's face. The quick glance of compassion she'd turned towards Lily before confirming to the others that her search of the witch had shown no sign of the Ouroboros. She'd sacrificed herself knowing that Lily held the means to save her.

And she could still save her. She could make it all right.

Lily clutched that thought to her like a life buoy as she closed her eyes. Focusing on the weight of the Ouroboros, she opened her mind to its energy and prayed. *This time it would work.*

5

The sun was setting low on the horizon as Phoenix pulled her Mustang up outside Ethan's apartment and cut the engine. The converted warehouse was surrounded on three sides by the docks, and the lights of the city reflected like a mirage on the water, ebbing and flowing with the tide.

She cast her eyes towards Abi in the passenger seat and noticed her friend absently picking at her nails. The drive there had been unusually quiet, and attempts at conversation had been met with distracted, one-word answers. The strange atmosphere was making Phoenix antsy.

It wasn't the first time Abi had come with her to Ethan's place. Ever since Abi had gotten a crash course on the Lore, they'd all made a conscious effort to ensure she was as comfortable in their world as possible, Ethan especially. And now that Phoenix thought about it, Abi had asked to come; she'd even organised cover for the bar. So, she had no reason to be nervous.

Then why did this suddenly feel like a very bad idea?

"Come on. The others will be waiting." She flashed Abi

a reassuring smile and climbed out into the chill of the evening. There'd be time enough to question her friend's strange mood later; first, she had a lecture to face.

Ethan had called two days ago to fill her in on the update from Cormac. It had been clear from his tone that he had his knickers in a twist, and she'd resigned herself to yet another argument about her safety. It didn't stop her putting him off ... or winding him up a little.

The memory of his frustrated growl when she'd regrettably informed him she wouldn't be free for a group meeting until Saturday brought a smile to her face. She could even picture the small muscle at the side of his jaw that was no doubt twitching as he ground his teeth together.

As much as she wanted to though, she couldn't put him off forever.

The rich smell of coffee beckoned her through the door of the upper floor apartment and into the open-plan living room where she found the others already assembled. Nate was perched on the edge of the leather sofa. His floppy brown hair fell into his amber eyes as he leaned over something that looked suspiciously like a Rubik's cube. The tech-loving shifter gestured excitedly to the vampire beside him as he held the object up for closer inspection, completely oblivious to the new arrivals.

Not impressed by Nate's enthusiasm, Shade slouched in the corner of the sofa with a surly expression held firmly in place. As she walked further into the room, his icy blue eyes flicked to her and the temperature seemed to drop to Arctic conditions.

She gave the vampire her friendliest smile, just for the satisfaction of making his scowl deepen.

A further survey found Lily at the large oak dining table with a mug clasped in her hands and a vacant expression on her face. The sight of the young witch pulled Phoenix up short.

Lily had seemed haggard when she'd last seen her a few days ago, but now she looked like she hadn't slept in weeks. The circles under her eyes had grown darker and appeared almost black in the dim light, and her once lustrous blonde hair hung unwashed in a limp ponytail.

Phoenix bit her lip and frowned.

At only eighteen years of age, Lily had seen more death than anyone should ever have to. The passing of her sister had hit the hardest, though. Phoenix could still remember Lily's anguished scream when Ethan broke the news to her. And yet somehow, Lily had shoved all of her grief aside to focus on helping them stop Darius and the witches.

But the thing about grief was that it couldn't be ignored forever. Eventually, it found its way to the surface. And it seemed like the toll was now beginning to show.

She pulled her eyes away from the young witch to look at Ethan, who stood with his back to the panoramic window that spanned the length of the room. A rough coat of stubble covered his jaw, highlighting the tense set of muscles as he, too, watched Lily. When he finally turned his gaze towards her, his brown eyes echoed her own concern, and Phoenix couldn't help but notice that he, too, looked worn out.

Behind her, Abi cleared her throat. "Hi," she said with a pointed wave.

As if a spell had been broken, everyone snapped into action, rearranging themselves to make space for the new arrivals. Phoenix plonked herself between Nate and Abi on the sofa, causing Shade to move to one of the lone recliners with a glare in her direction. Ethan joined Lily on the smaller two-seater – not that his choice of seat mattered to Phoenix.

"Okay, so we know the Council were due to meet last night," Ethan started, bringing the low murmur of conversation to a halt. "My dad hasn't been able to reach William, and he needs to tread carefully in case the Council find out about our involvement. So, for now, we're on our own."

Phoenix pointedly ignored the piercing stare he directed at her and the uneasy flutter in her stomach.

"The Council called that meeting for a reason," he continued. "Vicktor will have told them about you, even if he hasn't told them about the prophecy – which I think we can assume he has. It's not safe, Phoenix, and the longer you stay in Dublin, the more dangerous it becomes."

She blew out an exasperated breath, tired of the broken record. "Why should I run? I haven't done anything wrong."

Shade snorted and sat forward to rest his forearms on his knees. His icy blue eyes held hers, the challenge clear. "Do you really think it matters? Your very existence calls into question their authority. An inter-species relationship allowed to continue and produce offspring? If the Lore find out about you, the Council will appear weak. Do you really think they'll let that happen?"

The rebuttal stuck in her throat. Phoenix knew he was right, but still she rallied against the idea of being punished for something completely out of her control. Their edict was bullshit anyway; her parents had loved each other more than anyone she'd ever known.

Ethan stayed silent, watching her as she battled the conflicting emotions churning in her gut. She didn't want to face the Council – she really didn't – but she wasn't leaving. They had no right to make her.

Abi reached out to give her hand a squeeze. "What will happen to Phoenix if the Council does come?"

"It's hard to say," Ethan answered. "We've got no precedent for this situation, but the Council doesn't tend to look kindly on anything that threatens the order of things."

"And Phoenix does that?"

Ethan nodded.

Abi turned to her, still gripping her hand, and Phoenix felt her heart drop. Her friend's face was tight with worry; she knew immediately this was why Abi had come. Tonight had been a carefully orchestrated setup.

"Why are you still here?"

The question was rhetorical, of course. Abi was smart enough to figure out the answer for herself, but it hung in the air between them.

After they'd met Vicktor, the CLO rep, Ethan had convinced her to go stay with his pack in Donegal. She'd been so afraid she'd lose her parents all over again if they were forced to face the Council. Well, she lost them anyway. And when Darius took Abi, he'd shown her just how much more she stood to lose.

"The pack's offer of protection still stands. It wasn't solely for the benefit of your parents." Ethan's voice was gentle, his gaze sympathetic, but the determined set to his jaw remained.

"As long as Abi stays in Dublin, I'm staying." It wasn't up for debate. She wouldn't leave her friend vulnerable again.

All eyes in the room turned to Abi. Her hand tightened in Phoenix's and she squirmed under their scrutiny.

"Have we had any luck locating Darius?" Phoenix asked, attempting to divert the focus from her friend. She knew how hard Abi had worked to build herself up from nothing. She'd never ask her to leave.

"Afraid not," Nate answered, his tone a mix of frustration and admiration. "I don't know how they're doing it, but the vamps are doing a damn good job of covering his trail."

"Are you sure he's still alive? That sun trick of yours did a lot of damage." Shade tilted his head and considered her.

She pulled her hand away from Abi and clasped it with her other hand in her lap, suddenly conscious of the damage they were capable of. "He's alive."

"What about the Council?" Abi looked at Ethan. "If Vicktor tells them about Phoenix, he'll tell them about Darius too. Surely they should be the ones to deal with him?"

The room fell silent.

What she said made sense – logically, at least. But the tension that filled the room spoke volumes. The Council was powerful and also unpredictable. Phoenix didn't know about the others, but she could think of a million things she'd prefer to do than rely on that group of megalomaniacs for her safety. Like play Russian roulette. With explosive silver bullets.

She blew out a slow breath and forced the thoughts of Darius from her mind. *Good old Uncle D.* It was still hard to hear his name without feeling a lance of pain through her very core. She'd tried in vain to reconcile the monster with the man she'd once known, but it still didn't make sense to her. Hopefully, the scars she'd given him were as long-lasting as the ones he'd left on her heart.

"What's our next step with the prophecy?" she asked, grasping for something practical, though no less terrifying, to deal with.

Ethan tried to focus on the conversation around him, but his gaze kept slipping back to Phoenix. She might've thought that redirecting the discussion would get her off the hook, but she was very wrong. He'd lock her in the apartment if needed. She wasn't getting out of here until she saw sense.

He'd hoped that asking Abi along would help him. Play the guilt card a bit. He even thought he was onto a winner for one whole, precious minute, but he'd underestimated how closely linked Phoenix's actions were to her friend's.

Even with Abi on his side, he wasn't confident their combined pressure would be enough to get Phoenix to leave, at least not while Abi stayed behind. Hell, if he was honest with himself, he could mostly understand why she was being stubborn. Maybe even respected her for it. Unfortunately, respect wasn't going to keep her alive.

With a huff of frustration, he cracked his neck and stood; he needed some space to clear his head. After a quick pit stop in the kitchen to top up the refreshments – minus Shade's bag of blood, didn't want to freak out the human – he headed to the bathroom at the end of the hall to take a leak.

As he washed his hands and splashed water over his face, a sound came from the hallway.

Can't a man get two minutes peace?

He opened the door and pulled up short when he found Abi in the hall, her hands nervously entwining as she stared towards the bathroom.

"Sorry, did you need to –" He moved aside and indicated for her to go ahead, but she didn't budge.

A battle waged behind her blue eyes, and a sudden sense of unease set his Spidey senses tingling. "Abi, is everything okay?"

She opened her mouth to respond, but closed it again and shook her head.

"Is there somewhere we can talk that we won't be overheard?" She looked towards the living area and bit her lip.

The sense of unease grew stronger. He moved past her to open the door on the opposite side of the hall and, with a gentle hand on her back, ushered her into his bedroom. The door closed with a soft click behind them and he sat down on the bed, waiting for her to speak.

For a time, she simply paced.

The room wasn't small by any standards, but the super-king size bed and wall of wardrobes left little space for her to manoeuvre before she had to turn around again. He watched her with a detached fascination and wondered if there would be a path worn in the plush navy carpet by the time she finished.

"I should be talking to Phoenix about this, but I'm afraid if I tell her … I told myself there was no point saying anything. I mean, Darius was obviously crazy, right? And once he was gone, I just figured everything would go back to normal. The whole thing seemed so surreal. I didn't really think –"

She wrung her hands and turned to face him.

"Phoenix has to die."

6

Jaded by the conversation, Phoenix slumped back against the large cushions behind her. They were going around in circles, and everyone was starting to snipe at each other.

Well, actually, Nate and Shade were starting to snipe at each other. Lily stayed quiet, staring off into space, unless she was asked a direct question, and Abi still hadn't come back from the bathroom. How long did it take to pee, anyway?

A niggle of concern crept down her spine and she pushed herself up from the groove she'd settled into. No one even looked her way as she slipped out of the living room and made her way down the hall.

She was just about to call out to Abi and offer to send a search party when she noticed the bathroom door was ajar. Low murmuring came from the room on the opposite side of the hall, and she stared at the closed door of Ethan's bedroom.

Now that she'd become aware of the clandestine conversation, Abi and Ethan's voices were clearly distinguishable. A pang of something she didn't want to examine too closely caused her stomach to do a little flip-flop.

What the hell was going on?

They spoke quietly, so she moved closer to the door, mentally ordering her internal narrative to shut up so she could hear what was being said. The distress in Abi's voice was clear even before the words became audible. When they did, Phoenix's heart stopped cold.

"That's what he said. The only way to prevent the prophecy is for Phoenix to die."

A buzzing sound filled her ears and the narrow hallway closed in on her. Whatever was said after that was lost as her head spun and her vision blurred.

The funny thing was, she'd known. Some part of her deep down had known. Sure, hadn't she even used the threat of ending her own life against Darius.

But to hear the words out loud …

The bedroom door swung open and Phoenix found herself face to face with Ethan. The small muscle in his jaw was hopping, and the earlier image she'd had didn't seem so funny anymore. Behind him, Abi sat on the bed, looking dejected as she stared at the ground.

The moment stretched forever, tangible and oppressive. Eventually, Abi raised her tear-filled eyes and whispered, "I'm sorry."

A heavy silence filled the living room, and Phoenix could feel their eyes burning into her. She pulled her knees to her chest and tried to make herself smaller in the black leather recliner that mirrored Shade's.

What were they expecting her to do? Scream? Cry? A small part of her actually wanted to laugh. But the rest? Well, that was just numb.

Ethan's announcement that they knew what the prophecy said had grabbed everyone's attention immediately. Even Lily, in her subdued state, had jerked her head up in surprise. The same question came from everyone's lips: "How?"

How indeed.

Abi cast a pained glance in her direction before repeating the explanation she'd given Ethan in the bedroom.

"When Darius ... had me, he spoke about the prophecy. Gloated might be more accurate." Abi shuddered, a haunted look darkening her red-rimmed eyes. "He liked to play head games to show he could hurt me without even touching me. He took great pleasure in informing me that the only way to stop the prophecy was for Phoenix to die."

She spoke the last words softly, but every one of them was like a blade slicing through Phoenix's skin.

"So, if Ethan had killed her to start with," Shade said, his voice cold, "this would already be over."

The answering growl from Ethan made the hairs stand up on the back of Phoenix's arms. But she didn't need him to defend her because Shade was right. Her death would've stopped it all. Annabelle's murder. Abi's torture. Her parents' sacrifice. All of it had been for nothing.

"Oh no you don't." Ethan pointed a warning finger at her, glaring. "You don't get to play martyr in this."

She opened her mouth to argue, but before she could speak, Nate jumped up from the sofa, his hands held up in surrender.

"How about we get all the details before anyone goes making any rash decisions?" He looked pointedly at Shade and Ethan, then her before turning his attention to Abi. "Did Darius say anything else? Anything at all that might help us?"

"There was a scroll. It looked pretty old and had some kind of wax seal on it. I couldn't make out the seal properly, but it seemed familiar, like a scales or –"

"The Council," Lily whispered.

Phoenix's stomach dropped, and she swallowed back the bile that forced its way up her throat.

"Shit." Shade let out a low whistle and leaned back in his seat.

Abi looked around, her brow furrowed in confusion. "What does that mean? Is Darius working with the Council?"

"Not necessarily." Nate flicked his hair out of his eyes and started pacing as he worked through his thoughts. "We found texts on the prophecy in the Council archives, so we knew they were aware of it."

"How did Darius get the scroll if he's not working with them?"

Nate shrugged. "There was no mention of a scroll in anything I found. There was reference to someone named Cassandra, the Horsemen, and a tearing of the fabric that protects our world. That's all."

"Terror, destruction, death to man. The fires of hell o'ertake the land." Abi's voice shook as she spoke the words. Everyone froze.

"What did you say?" Ethan leaned forward, barely contained urgency visible in the tension that ran from the hunched muscles of his upper back to his clasped fists.

"That was what the scroll said. Or at least, how Darius read it." Abi stared into the distance, her nose scrunching in concentration. "So long as she alone does stand, shall the Horsemen walk the land. There may have been more but..." She shook her head, tears glistening in her eyes as her shoulders slumped. "I'm sorry. I should have said something."

A strange sense of detachment settled over Phoenix, leaving her cold and numb all at the same time. It hurt to see the look of regret on her friend's face, and a part of her wanted nothing more than to wrap her arms around Abi and tell her it'd be all right. But she couldn't. Because Abi's words had forced her to face the truth she'd been ignoring: It wasn't over.

For the past few weeks, her parent's death had given her something to focus on other than the stupid prophecy, and she'd let herself wallow in the haze of grief. She'd become complacent. Even with the nightly patrols, and the work she'd been doing on her fae powers, she'd forgotten what was really at stake. She'd taken each demon possession as an inconvenience to be dealt with rather than a sign of what was to come.

"How long?" she asked, her tongue like sandpaper in her mouth. "Did the scroll say how long we have?"

"When the clock strikes midnight on your twenty-fifth year."

Ten months. A lot of innocent people could die in ten months.

Phoenix pushed herself up from the recliner, suddenly feeling like the room was shrinking around her. "Nate, you mind if I go patrolling with you tonight?"

Ethan was in front of her in a flash. His hands gripped her upper arms and his expression pleaded with her. "We have time to figure this out. Promise me you won't do anything stupid."

A tight nod was the only answer she gave before she yanked her body out of his grip and grabbed her leather jacket from the back of the chair. She pulled her car keys from her pocket and threw them to Abi.

"I'll be home late."

With that, she made her way to the door, not waiting to see if Nate followed.

7

The buzzing in Lily's head grew louder as she watched Ethan pace the living room. Without a word, she stood from her chair and squeezed past Shade. His eyes followed her as she left, but she ignored him. She needed to get out of there.

First stop was her bedroom. She locked the door quietly behind her before lifting her mattress to retrieve the Ouroboros, still tucked away safely in the wooden box. She averted her eyes so as not to see the photo on the lid, but Annabelle's smiling face drew her gaze back like a magnet she couldn't resist. Bitterness welled up inside her, making her gut roil painfully.

No one called after her as she slipped out of the apartment without bothering to grab a jacket. No one noticed.

The night was icy cold as she walked along the docks, focusing only on her breath as it fogged the air in front of her and the burn of the wind against her face. The cold was an anaesthetic and she welcomed it.

For so long, she'd let the guilt eat away at her. Night

after night she'd lie in bed, thinking of the people who had sacrificed themselves so she could have the Ouroboros. But what about her? What about what she'd sacrificed?

With Abi's words, the guilt had changed. It was shifting around inside of her, morphing into something alien and terrifying.

None of it mattered. The sacrifices, the Ouroboros, the chance to fix things. All of it was pointless. Because Phoenix still lived. And as long as she lived, the rest of them would continue to suffer.

She walked for a while, trying to sort through the screaming thoughts that fought for attention in her head, and when she looked up, she was surprised to find herself at a busy junction near O'Connell Street.

How had she gotten there? She didn't recall walking so far.

A car horn blared, and she leapt back to avoid being splashed as a car drove straight into a puddle at her feet. Lily muttered a curse under her breath and slipped through a break in traffic to the safety of a nearby footpath, drenched and freezing. The few pedestrians passing by gawked at her as if she was crazy. And who knew? Maybe they were right.

A small cafe sat on the corner, and the soft lights beckoned her like a lighthouse. She pushed open the chipped wooden door to the sound of jingling bells, and the rich aroma of caffeine engulfed her senses.

The clock on the wall indicated that it was near closing, and the cafe was empty of customers. Still, the kindly old woman behind the counter ushered her to a table and placed a cup of steaming coffee in front of her. She shook her head when Lily tried to dig some money out of her jeans pocket and gave her a pat on the shoulder before returning to her cleaning.

Lily clutched the cup in her hands and waited for the heat to sink in. But the cold she felt wasn't physical, and it wasn't one that could be fixed with a cup of coffee.

So many people dead. Not just Annabelle, others too. Was Shade right? Could all of those people have been saved if Ethan had just killed Phoenix in the beginning? How many more would die now? Even if she managed to use the Ouroboros, it wouldn't matter; she'd be dooming her sister all over again. There was no happy ending for any of them. Not while Phoenix was alive.

She reached down to the bag that sat by her feet and drew out the wooden box. It felt heavier than normal as she placed it on the table. The photo on the lid lost focus as tears burned her eyes.

"Please, Annie, tell me what to do," she whispered, scrunching her eyes shut.

8

Ethan's gaze followed Phoenix around the pub as he tapped his foot absently in time to the band's music. His pint of Blue Moon sat untouched on the wooden table in front of him, and the paper beer coaster was in shreds beside it instead of absorbing the condensation that ran down the glass.

"Has she spoken to you?" Abi asked as appeared beside him. Her line of sight followed his as she twisted a cloth in her hands.

"Just to inform me she doesn't need a babysitter and that everything is fine."

"Ooooo."

Ethan laughed. He'd grown up around enough women to know that when a woman told you it was "fine", you were in deep shit.

It didn't help that he had no clue why Phoenix was pissed at him. But based on the ice-cold welcome he'd received, she obviously was. His arrival that evening had been met with a dagger stare, and she'd spent the entire night avoiding him.

He'd watched her from a distance as she laughed and joked with the other customers. A general observer would be fooled into thinking she was happy and relaxed, but he could see the telltale tension in her shoulders. Hell, he could almost see the steam coming from her ears.

"You?" He noted the tightness around Abi's eyes and the frown that creased her forehead, already guessing the answer.

Abi blew a strand of hair out of her face with a sigh. "I waited up last night to talk to her, but I guess it was a late one."

She looked at him for confirmation, but he looked away, not quite meeting her gaze as he gave a non-committal grunt. Nate had gotten home from patrol some-time around midnight, so Phoenix should have been the same. She obviously needed space to process everything, and the last thing he wanted to do was add to Abi's concerns, so he figured silence was the lesser evil in this case.

His phone buzzed on the table, and he gave her an apologetic smile as he noted his father's name on the screen. Leaving his full pint behind, he slipped outside to take the call.

"Have you managed to get in touch with William?" he asked, foregoing all forms of pleasantries.

"Is that any way to greet your Alpha?" Cormac growled. "Or your father?"

Ethan closed his eyes and took a breath. His father wasn't the bad guy here; all he'd done was try to help. It wasn't Cormac's fault a certain redhead put him in a bad mood.

"Sorry, it's been a long few days. We got more information on the prophecy."

"Nothing good I take it?" Cormac's voice softened, no trace of the Alpha remaining, only a father's concern.

Ethan shook his head even though his father couldn't see him. He had no idea how to start explaining the clusterfuck they were in or the heavy weight of dread Abi's words had triggered.

"Ethan?"

"Yeah, sorry, I'm still here. It turns out Darius had a scroll."

In concise, emotionless detail, he brought Cormac up to speed. He forced himself to focus only on the facts; the implication spoke for itself.

For a minute, there was silence.

"We have time, son. We'll find another way."

The words struck Ethan in a place he wasn't ready to examine yet, and he swiftly changed the subject. "What about the Council? Did you speak to William?"

"He seems to have fallen off the radar since the meeting." Even through the phone, Cormac's frustration was palpable.

"Maybe if I try to contact him?"

"And say what? He expects me to take an interest in Council business. It's my job as Alpha. If you start asking questions, you'll only draw attention to yourself."

"So, I'll tell him the truth."

The line fell silent once more.

"Make no mistake, Ethan," Cormac said, finally,

"William's loyalty is to the Council. The fact you're family will mean nothing to him if he believes your actions pose a risk to the Lore."

Ethan's free hand clenched. They'd had this argument before and he just couldn't understand it. Family came first. Always. Besides, if Vicktor had informed the Council of his meeting, there was every chance he'd mentioned the wolf by Phoenix's side. That alone would be enough to raise questions. It would be better if William heard the truth from him.

"Think carefully, son. If the Council knows of your connection to the hybrid, you put the whole pack at risk. Are you ready to ask that of them?"

An uncomfortable knot settled in the pit of Ethan's stomach, and he cursed. "I have to go. Let me know if you hear anything from William."

He hung up and shoved the phone into his pocket, biting back a roar of frustration. His father was right. Whether he liked it or not, anything he did reflected on the pack. It didn't matter how far he ran from his responsibilities.

With that thought gnawing at him, he turned to go back into the pub, only to find himself face to face with Phoenix. Her vivid green eyes were unreadable as she watched him with her arms folded tightly across her chest.

"I don't need you to save me, Ethan."

His jaw dropped. Was that what she thought he was trying to do? Play the knight in shining armour?

"I know you're trying to help," she continued, tone cooler than he'd heard from her since they first met. "But I'm a big girl, and I can look out for myself."

His anger flared. She was so bloody stubborn. Did she not realise it was going to get her killed?

"And what about the people that get hurt while you're busy looking out for yourself?" He growled and pushed past her, stalking into the night.

***

As Ethan's form disappeared from sight, Phoenix bit back the urge to scream. Frustration mixed with anger, churning into a mess of emotions that crawled over her skin. He didn't get to push her around or decide what was best for her. She'd done fine before he came along; there was no need for his self-sacrificing bullshit. She wasn't asking anyone to put themselves in danger for her. She didn't *want* them to put themselves in danger for her.

The anger wrapped around her like a protective armour and she yanked open the door of the pub. Even from across the room, she could feel Abi's concerned gaze boring into her. She pointedly ignored it and set about cleaning tables. She didn't need their concern ... or their pity.

The night passed in a blur and by closing time, her mood had only marginally improved. She'd avoided Abi by using customers as live body-shields and had multiple arguments with Ethan in her head – all of which she won, naturally. But as the last stragglers slipped out the door, she saw Abi approach from the corner of her eye.

"Ethan left in a bit of a rush earlier. Is everything okay?"

An uncomfortable knot of jealousy twisted in her stomach, adding more fuel to her anger. Why was Abi so concerned about Ethan all of a sudden?

"Everything's fine. I just made it clear I didn't need him to babysit me." She moved to the side but Abi blocked her way, unyielding.

"He's worried about you. Why is that so bad?"

"I don't need him to be worried about me. I don't need everyone to protect me." She glared pointedly at her friend but was met with defiant blue eyes.

"Does it ever cross your bloody mind that we care about you?"

"Oh, so you kept the truth from me because you cared?"

"Yes! Just like you kept the truth from me because you cared." With that, Abi turned on her heel and disappeared through the door that led to their apartment.

Phoenix stared after her, an uncomfortable burning sensation building in the back of her throat. What was she doing? She didn't want to argue with Abi. Or anyone, really. It was like she couldn't stop herself. The sane part of her brain was being held hostage, nothing more than a muffled voice trying to make itself heard through the haze that was clogging her head.

She should be upstairs with Abi right now, curled up on the sofa, debating which tacky movie to watch tonight. Instead, there was this huge divide between them – one she'd created. And she didn't know how to fix it.

With a heaviness in her heart, she locked the doors and trudged upstairs to her room. The first thing she saw when she switched on the light was the wooden box resting on her locker. The subtle fragrance of herbs reached her, and an image of her parents flashed before her eyes. They'd given up so much for her. And it was all for nothing.

She crumpled to the floor and let the silent tears flow.

9

Darius sank into the plush velvet couch that had been handcrafted specially to fit the curved office and regarded the man across from him. To his right, a floor-to-ceiling window offered a panoramic view of the club below and the sea of writhing bodies that filled the dancefloor. On his left, a bank of monitors covered the wall.

Each screen was connected to a security camera in one of the private rooms below the club. At this time of night, the rooms would all be occupied, but the monitors remained silent and black; he didn't think his guest would quite appreciate the show they provided.

He took a sip of his whiskey and leaned back in the chair. "You have news for me?"

Vicktor nodded and pulled a handkerchief from his pocket, grimacing as he not-so-discreetly wiped his hands. A glass of whiskey sat untouched in front of him. Amused, Darius noted the stiff set of his shoulders as he avoided looking towards the club.

"This is an interesting place you have here."

Darius smiled at the undertone of disdain in Vicktor's voice. "We like to cater for all tastes ... Even those not necessarily to our liking."

A non-committal grunt was the only answer as Vicktor wiped his hands once more.

"The witches are going in tonight."

Darius stilled.

"Where?"

The other man eyed him warily. "Does it really matter? She's either strong enough to survive the hit or she's not."

Darius leaned forward, allowing himself a moment to imagine ripping Vicktor's throat out. "Humour me."

"I'll give you this information, but then I'm out, Darius. I won't betray the Council any more than I already have – even if they are misguided."

Darius took another sip of his drink, using the glass to mask his impatience.

"The hovel she calls a home. They're on their way now."

That didn't give him long to act.

With an amicable smile, Darius pushed himself to standing. "I appreciate you coming here to tell me." He brushed his hands down the front of his jacket, smoothing out the soft cashmere. "Now, I'm afraid you'll have to excuse me; I have another prior arrangement. My guards will be happy to show you out. Unless you wish to stay and partake in the entertainment?"

His smile shifted, and with pleasure, he noticed the other man flinch before he turned and left the viewing room.

10

What the –

Phoenix's eyes shot open. The insistent tapping that had pervaded her dreams continued. Darkness filled the room around her, and in her groggy state it took a moment to realise the noise wasn't just a figment of her imagination.

She rolled over to look at the window where red eyes stared back at her through the glass. A scream bubbled up in her throat.

The crow's loud squawk broke through the terror long enough to make her pause. Even against the backdrop of night, the bird's feathers were a miasma of colours that rippled hypnotically as they ruffled in the wind.

Red eyes. Feathers like an oil-slick rainbow. She'd seen this bird before.

The crow's tapping became more frantic and its squawk more insistent. She scooched up in the bed until her back was against the headboard, but kept her eyes glued to the window. Surely it couldn't be the same bird? The one that had saved her from the first demon?

Apparently satisfied to have gotten her attention, the crow took flight and disappeared in a blur of feathers.

Well, that wasn't creepy.

Shaken, she looked around her room, half expecting the bogeyman to jump out at her next. What she saw instead stopped her short.

A thin wisp of smoke seeped under the bedroom door and moved across the floor like fog. She sniffed the air but found no smell of burning, and the fire alarm was noticeably silent. She closed her eyes and peeked one eye open, but the smoke was still there, thicker now.

Shit! Abi.

Panic sent a spike of adrenaline through her. She leapt out of bed and ran to the door, yanking it open before her brain belatedly reminded her to check how warm it was.

The hallway beyond was a haze of smoke, a strange blue hue trailing along the ground behind it. A wisp of the smoke touched her bare legs and creeped upward in a tender caress. A light prickle of static followed its path over her skin, but aside from that odd sensation, there was nothing.

No smell. No immediate clogging of her airways. None of the things that should have come with smoke.

Abi's room was barely twenty feet from where she stood, yet in that moment it felt like miles. She sprinted down the hall and yanked the door open, not bothering to knock. The room was filled with the strange blue smoke, and she could only just make out Abi's form lying in the bed. Unmoving.

Phoenix's heart stuttered and clenched painfully. In the

split second it took her to reach the bed, she did something she hadn't ever done before: she prayed.

She'd be a better person, a better friend. She'd stop being a complete pain in the arse. She'd forgive her friend for every little lie and apologise for her own glaringly obvious double standards. She'd do anything.

The rise and fall of Abi's breathing was so subtle that, for a moment, she thought she was imagining it. Phoenix placed her hand on her friend's chest and when she felt the gentle movement, she let out a sob of relief.

"Abi." She shook the still form. "Abi."

No answer.

Panic started to overtake her once more and she shook harder. Still no response. Then, through the haze of smoke and fear, she heard it: footsteps.

She darted to the door and crouched low. Tentatively, she peered into the empty hallway.

The footsteps grew louder and a second later, a man stepped into view at the top of the staircase. Long robes draped over his lanky frame, and a trail of blue flames followed in his wake like an eager puppy lapping at his heels. His lips moved in a silent chant and his signature washed over her, bringing with it a burning heat.

The flame crawled up the walls, slowly devouring everything it touched. Everything except the witch.

She cursed and glanced towards the bed. The witch would reach her in seconds, and the only other exit from the bedroom was a small window with a two-storey drop. Could she make it without hurting her friend?

There was no time to decide, however, as the witch began to walk in her direction.

Without thinking, she lunged from her crouched position at the door and barrelled into him. He stumbled a couple of feet, but his mouth turned up in a satisfied smile as his eyes fell on her.

Blue fire surrounded them both in an instant, and Phoenix was consumed by a heat so intense it could sear the flesh from her bones. Her instincts screamed at her to run.

Instead, she drew closer to the witch until she found herself within his protective sphere and the heat reduced somewhat. Unfortunately, it also brought her within reaching distance.

The witch grabbed at her, but she twisted away, using her speed to her advantage. The close quarter training sessions Ethan had forced on her suddenly seemed a lot more relevant now.

Conscious of the flames growing closer and closer to Abi, she waited for an opening. The witch was strong, but a significant portion of his energy was focused on creating the magic fire and eventually she saw her opportunity.

A sharp jab to the kidney doubled him over in pain and she followed through with a knee to the jaw. The strike caught at the perfect angle and he fell to the floor, unconscious.

Blue flame flared up along the narrow strip of floor between her and the witch. She stumbled back, raising her arms in front of her face in a vain attempt to shield from the heat. Every instinct in her body screamed to finish off the witch; he'd come into her home and threatened the safety of the people she loved. He couldn't be allowed to live.

But even with the witch unconscious, the flames continued to spread. Gaping holes appeared in the plasterboard that coated the walls, exposing wooden beams that were quickly turning black. There was no time. She needed to get Abi out.

With a final look towards the witch, she ran back to Abi's room and lifted her friend carefully from the bed. Hoisting her over her shoulder, Phoenix shoved back the panic that rose like bile in her throat.

The rise and fall of Abi's chest was shallower now, her breathing laboured. Phoenix was suddenly aware of the tightness in her own lungs. Each inhale caused an ache of protest between her ribs and burned a path down her windpipe.

Abi wasn't much smaller than her, and though her friend's weight was easily manageable, the mechanics of carrying a person proved difficult. She risked a quick glance into the hallway on the off-chance of an easier escape route, but when she saw the witch begin to stir, she turned back to the window with a grimace.

A single, full-force kick and the glass shattered. The gust of wind that blew through the opening caused the fire to explode into a violent furnace behind her. She ignored the shards of glass that stuck into her bare feet and took a running leap, clutching Abi tight to her.

The jarring thud as she hit the ground sent her tumbling, and she barely managed to twist enough to protect her friend from the fall.

An abnormal blue hue filled the night around her. The sounds of nearby yelling had her on her feet and running within seconds. She didn't look back. Not once. Not even when a loud explosion shattered her hopes of ever returning home.

11

Darius snapped the neck of the second witch just as an upper-storey window exploded and a flash of red leapt through the night. He watched as Phoenix rolled and stumbled to her feet with a pale, human-sized form clutched in her arms.

The fucking human? He snarled. Had he taught her nothing about her weaknesses?

Three more witches still surrounded the pub; their yells confirming they, too, had spotted her. He moved in a blur, careful to keep to the shadows as he tore out their jugulars one after the other and left them in a gurgling heap on the ground. Five down, one to go.

Behind him, blue fire continued to devour the building, casting an eerie halo into the night. That meant the sixth witch was still alive. And powerful, if the magic blaze was anything to go by. Vicktor hadn't pulled his punches when he arranged the hit.

From the shadows, he watched Phoenix adjust her human baggage and make a hasty retreat, no doubt heeding the previous yells as warning of further pursuit. Well, she needn't worry; he wasn't letting her die that easily.

Just as she cleared his line of sight, a pale face appeared at the broken window. Even with the distance between them, he could see the fury etched into the witch's features.

The man's descent from the upper floor was far more graceful than Phoenix's had been since he wasn't lugging an unnecessary weight with him. A black cloak billowed behind him as he landed on the ground in a crouch, a trail of blue flame following his descent.

The man stood, his tall frame creating an imposing silhouette against the backdrop of destruction. He glanced at his fallen comrades, then clicked his fingers. A loud explosion rippled through the night.

As he stalked into the darkness after Phoenix, Darius followed. Impressive as the man's powers were, he couldn't be allowed to live.

Stones ground into Phoenix's bare feet, pushing the shards of glass further in with each step. She gritted her teeth and bent her head against the biting wind that scorched her exposed skin.

Mental note: get more practical pyjamas.

The baggy t-shirt skimming her thighs offered little protection against the freezing February temperatures. Over her shoulder, she could feel the goosebumps covering Abi's ice-cold skin through the silk nightwear she wore. Her gut twisted as she added hypothermia to the list of possible things liable to kill them both before the night was over.

Abi hadn't stirred at all. Not when Phoenix had leapt with her from the first storey window, and not now as she was being jostled about like a ragdoll. She could only hope that her friend's slumber was some strange side-effect of the magic fire and would lift once she'd gotten them far enough from the source.

Tears pricked her eyes, but she forced herself to keep moving despite the sense of loss that threatened to choke her. The witch would be coming for her. Besides, there was nothing to turn back for; their home was gone.

The night was quiet and the streets empty. Anyone with an ounce of sanity had long ago succumbed to the safety of their beds, and for that, she was grateful. Still, she was conscious of being seen. A half-naked woman carrying another unconscious body would definitely raise some questions.

She looked around, debating her options. The shop fronts afforded her some shadow, but while she stayed on the main street, she was exposed. Soon, she'd run out of shops and hit the residential areas, which would only increase the likelihood of attracting attention. Not to mention the potential for collateral damage if the witch caught her.

At the end of the street, she turned the corner, and was debating her next move when a sound from the main street made her freeze. Her heart pounded so loudly that she had to concentrate to hear past it.

The sound came again, faint and almost imperceptible. The scuff of cloth against stones maybe? The witch's cloak?

Her fight-or-flight response sent a burst of adrenaline through her system, clearly voting to fight. But even as it did, her hands grasped reflexively, pulling Abi tighter. She couldn't fight like this.

Desperate, she looked around for somewhere to place her friend that would keep her out of the crossfire, but there was nothing but an empty path as far as the eye could see.

Another sound, louder this time, followed by a grunt.

With no other choice, she lowered Abi to the ground and edged cautiously along the wall, back the way she'd come. She paused at the corner, her body tense as she waited for the witch to appear.

A full minute passed, and nothing happened. Very slowly, she crouched down and peered around the corner.

The main street was empty, as silent as it had been when she'd made her way down it only minutes before. There was no sign of the witch and no material dragging along the ground. Was her imagination playing tricks on her?

She couldn't shake the feeling that someone would jump out at her any second, but when another survey of the street showed no movement, she ran back and hefted Abi over her shoulder once more. She needed to get help for her friend.

Turning another corner, she followed a winding path back to the main road. Hopefully, anyone following her would get fed up and go home ... *Yeah, because she'd be that lucky.*

She'd left the pub in such a hurry that she hadn't thought to grab her phone and she wracked her brain, trying desperately to remember Ethan's number – or if phone boxes even still existed. What other options did she have? Could she figure out a route that would get her to Ethan's apartment without attracting attention? Her chances were slim to none, and something told her Abi didn't have that much time.

She turned the final corner and barrelled straight into the broad chest of a shocked pedestrian. The man's expression was almost comical, eyes flitting between her and the body she carried as he instinctively took a step back. His mouth opened and closed multiple times before he managed to formulate any words.

"Are you okay?"

12

The red hue of dawn broke over the city horizon as Ethan stared out his living room window. His eyes were heavy with sleep, but his body was restless and his head wouldn't shut up. He'd gone to bed fuming after his fight with Phoenix, and the fact that he was awake at stupid o'clock only made his mood worse.

Nightmares had plagued him all night, each of them involving some kind of horrific death for Phoenix while he watched on, unable to act. The last had been the worst, and he'd woken in a pool of sweat with the image still burned into his mind: her walking into an inferno of blue flame, a serene smile on her face.

It was her fault, of course. He was only trying to help because he cared. If she wasn't so determined to push everyone away, she'd see that. Maybe he should just accept that he was fighting a losing battle?

His wolf growled at the suggestion and he dropped his head into his hands, letting out a low rumble of frustration. He was a bloody pushover.

Screw this. He grabbed his leather jacket from the back of the sofa and stood. After a quick check for the keys to his bike, he stalked out of the apartment, not bothering to lock the door behind him.

The matte black Harley sat waiting patiently for him just inside the shuttered doors of the converted warehouse. The mere sight of its sleek curves made him smile, and the tightness in his chest eased a little. He slipped on his jacket and pressed the button to raise the metal doors.

The cold morning air hit him and he took a deep breath, relishing the freshness. Maybe he'd head for the Wicklow Mountains. He'd been spending too much time in the city lately. His wolf was getting edgy.

Plan set, he swung his leg over the bike. His mobile phone chose that moment to start buzzing insistently, and he swore. Memories of his nightmares flashed through his mind as he struggled to free the phone from his jeans pocket and his body tensed.

The number on the screen was unfamiliar, and he hesitated with his finger over the answer button. A twist of anxiety in his gut refused to let him ignore it, however, so he brought the phone to his ear with a longing glance at the door.

"Ethan?" Phoenix's harried voice came down the line before he even had a chance to speak. "Yes, yes, I'll be quick," she said, voice muffled as she spoke to someone beside her.

In the background, he could hear a strange rhythmic beeping and wheels squeaking on linoleum.

"Phoenix? What's going on? Where are you?"

For a moment, she was quiet. The distant sound of

shouting reached him through the phone, followed by the sudden blaring of an alarm. A deep sense of dread hit him and his mouth dried as if filled with sawdust.

"I'm in the hospital," she finally answered, a sob choking its way free. "There was a fire."

The stench of disinfectant and disease assaulted Ethan as soon as he pushed through the doors of the hospital. The smell clawed its way down the back of his throat, nearly choking him. Everything was white and sterile, from the walls, to the floors, to the people, and he shuddered at the cloud of death that hung in every fibre of the place.

Phoenix had assured him on the phone that both she and Abi were okay, but his pounding heart refused to calm until he saw for himself.

A quick glance at the overhead signs pointed him in the direction of their ward. He ignored the protests from the hospital security guard as he took the first right turn and ran down the corridor.

Even at the early hour, the hospital was a buzz of activity; workers hurried past him in scrubs, their expressions varying between haggard, determined, or a mix of both. The occasional patient shuffled about in their dressing gown, and a young couple sat on distorted plastic chairs, clutching hands as they sobbed. They all ignored him, focused only on whatever situation had brought them there.

He knew he'd found the right room when he turned a corner and spotted two uniformed Gardaí talking quietly outside a closed door. Both seemed too young to shave, let alone guard anything, but their presence gave him pause.

Phoenix hadn't mentioned the police when she rang. Their involvement probably stood to reason given the fire, but surely they didn't need to be at the hospital?

As he approached the room, he waited for them to stop him and question his presence since visiting time wasn't for another three hours, at least. Instead, they both gave him a sympathetic look and nodded politely before moving to the side to allow him clear access to the door.

It was then he noticed the sound of arguing coming from the room, and he groaned as he realised just what the sympathy was for. Phoenix's stubborn tone was as familiar to him as his own by now, and in a strange way, it eased some of the tension that had been bubbling up inside.

He braced himself and pushed open the door to find her sitting on a stiff metal chair beside a hospital bed that looked equally comfortable. A dirty t-shirt was the only thing covering her and blood coated her feet. Other than that, she appeared unharmed. Abi sat propped up by pillows in the bed and though her skin had a slightly grey tinge to it, her blue eyes were alert and sparkling with barely restrained laughter.

"I told you, I'm fine. I don't need to be checked out." Phoenix looked up as he stepped into the room and gestured desperately towards an old man in a white coat who stood glaring at her from the end of the bed. "Ethan, can you please tell this nice doctor that I said thank you, but I don't require his assistance? He doesn't seem to want to listen to me."

Before he could say anything, the doctor tapped his

clipboard pointedly, nodding towards her feet. "It says here you had broken glass in your feet; you may need stitches.

"Nope, no stitches needed here," she insisted, crossing her arms over her chest and tucking her feet under her on the chair. Her jaw was set firm, but her eyes were pleading as she turned to him for help.

He couldn't stop the smile that caused his lip to quirk up as he watched her squirm. A small part of him was so tempted to draw it out. But she was right, of course. They couldn't let the doctor check her out. Who knew what their human tests would show, or wouldn't show, as the case may be.

With an apologetic look back to the doctor, he shrugged. "Sorry, doc. She's a stubborn one."

The doctor shook his head and shoved the clipboard towards Phoenix. "If you insist on being so stupid, you'll need to sign this release to confirm you refused medical attention."

She took the clipboard from him and quickly scrawled her name before handing it back as if it might burn her.

"What about me, doctor?" Abi chimed in.

The man turned to her and frowned. "All of your tests have come back normal, but I'd like to keep you in for observation. Smoke inhalation can be very serious."

Abi nodded in understanding, then pushed the blanket off and swung her legs over the side of the bed, wearing nothing more than a paper-thin hospital gown. She looked around the room in confusion before turning to Phoenix.

"Don't suppose I've got any clothes here?"

Ethan handed over the rucksack that Phoenix had asked him to bring and politely averted his eyes to allow

Abi some degree of modesty. He'd borrowed the clothes from Lily, so they should more or less fit. Either way, they couldn't really be too picky right now.

"What are you doing?" the doctor spluttered as Abi pulled on a pair of blue jeans.

"Discharging myself." She gave him an innocent smile and continued dressing. "You said all of my tests were fine."

The man's face turned a worrying shade of red, and Ethan almost felt sorry for him. He obviously recognised a lost cause when he saw one, however, as he turned on his heel, muttering something about preparing the paperwork as he stalked from the room.

The moment the door closed and they were once more alone, Ethan shifted his attention to Phoenix. He scanned her from head to toe, the tension he felt only fully unravelling once he was satisfied she was unharmed. Dark circles ringed her eyes, and a subtle mix of fear and sorrow shadowed her features, but she seemed to be holding it together out of sheer stubbornness.

"Okay, what happened? Why are the police outside?"

In a toneless voice, she relayed the events of the night before: waking up to the blue flame, her battle with the witch, escaping with Abi. "Needless to say, the good Samaritan was a bit concerned about the fact I was carting around an unconscious body and called the police," she finished with a wry smile.

Memories from his nightmare flashed to mind – the blue flames, Phoenix's oddly serene smile, his sense of helplessness. He pushed the thought away with effort and forced himself to focus on the here and now.

"Have they questioned you?"

She nodded. "I managed to convince them that shock and adrenaline turned me into Superwoman, and that's how I was able to carry Abi to safety."

He snorted. It was amazing the things humans would believe while completely ignoring the obvious signs right in front of them. "Why are they still here? Is it because of the fire?"

Her cheeks coloured and she looked sheepish all of a sudden. Abi sniggered beside her.

"I may have had a minor argument with the doc when he tried to examine me. They said they have to wait for their boss to give them the go-ahead to leave, but I think they've been told to stick around in case I cause any trouble."

He put his head in his hand and took a deep breath. It had been a long night. The last thing they needed was to draw attention from the human authorities.

"Let's not give them reason to hang around any longer." He waved at the bag of clothes and indicated for her to follow Abi's lead and get changed.

He turned his back, mentally berating himself for the sudden urge to peek. Instead, he focused on the details of Phoenix's story. Blue flame equalled witch. A strong one. He had a hard time believing the witches themselves had organised the attack, which left Darius or the Council. Neither option was appealing.

When the rustling behind him stopped and the room fell silent, he deemed it safe to turn back around. Phoenix and Abi stood together watching him, both looking more vulnerable than he'd ever seen them before.

"Ready to go?" he asked gently.

Phoenix looked at Abi, her green eyes haunted.

"We have no place to go anymore."

Darius wove between the gathered Witnesses, drawing closer to the centre of the amphitheatre where Vicktor kneeled before the Council. Large candles bordered the raised platform upon which the five Council members stood, their hoods lowered. Shadows flitted across their impassive faces and he smiled in anticipation of their judgement.

Vicktor had kept the details of the attack short and sweet: pub burned down, casualties sustained, hybrid still alive. A heavy silence fell over the chamber in response to the news.

Vlad stepped forward, looking down at Vicktor with a sneer of disdain. "You say the witches are all dead?"

Vicktor hesitated a moment. "It would appear the hybrid got the upper hand on them."

Darius raised an eyebrow. *Is that so?*

"So, you failed."

A low murmur filled the chamber, and the room bristled with tension. Vicktor bowed his head in supplication before straightening up to look at each of the Council members in turn.

"It's true. I underestimated the hybrid. However, I have some information that may be of use to you, if you would allow me?"

Vlad opened his mouth to respond, but Méabh moved forward and placed a hand on his shoulder. Red-tipped nails dug into his flesh as she smiled. Even from his position in the crowd, Darius could see the barely restrained anger darken Vlad's eyes.

"Please proceed," she ordered Vicktor, the seductive invitation carrying a very clear warning.

Vicktor stood and gave Vlad a smug smile as he brushed down his grey suit, his sense of self-preservation obviously non-existent.

"A source has informed me that, aside from the wolf, there is also a witch keeping company with the hybrid. A young girl. I have it on good authority that the girl is a weak link you may be able to exploit."

There was a subtle shifting around the room at the news. Darius watched Diana, who had stayed silent to this point but tensed noticeably at the mention of witch involvement. He cast his mind back to the confrontation with Phoenix at his lair. Had there been a witch with her? He couldn't quite remember.

"Please elaborate," Méabh encouraged with a wave of her hand.

"It appears that the witch lost a sister. An unfortunate accident, so I'm told, but closely related to the issue of the prophecy. Loss can breed resentment, and if the hybrid is the only reason the prophecy exists ..."

"We may be able to turn this witch to our cause." Méabh tapped a viciously sharp fingernail against her lip as she regarded the CLO rep.

"You really think a young, inexperienced witch can succeed where your highly trained witches failed?" Vlad directed the question to Vicktor but arched his eyebrow in contempt at his fae co-Council.

"That's not what I'm proposing." Vicktor shook his head. "An unfortunate side-effect to the failed attack is that the hybrid will run. It'll make it a lot harder to kill her if you can't find her. This witch can provide you information about her location. I believe you already have the means to finish the job."

The whole room stilled, except for the shadows. At Vicktor's words, they began to swirl and twist, wrapping themselves around the Council before settling once more in the background.

Chills ran down Darius's spine and he shivered. Anticipation settled in his gut like a jolt of electricity. For a split second, he forgot that he, in fact, needed Phoenix alive, and he imagined the thrill of facing a true challenge again after so many centuries.

"You propose we call on the Mists." Kam cast a glance at the shadows behind him, his face expressionless.

Vicktor inclined his head.

The whole room seemed to hold its breath. In all the time Darius had acted as a Witness to the Council, he'd only seen the Mists deployed twice. The result had been a swift and sure end to the targets, despite the fact that both were Supes of immense power. The simple mention of the Council's assassins was enough to strike terror into the heart of all within the Lore, and their threat alone maintained order. Even the most powerful being couldn't fight what they couldn't touch.

The Council formed a circle, pulling up their blood red hoods as they turned their attention from the waiting crowd. Behind them, the shadows began to shift and take shape. Darius watched in fascination as, one by one, the Mists took their human form.

Two men and a woman stood in place of the shadows. Black harem pants and long, flowing robes covered most of their tanned skin, and hoods were pulled low over their head, shadowing their exotic features. But even in the darkness they used for cover, their eyes were clearly distinguishable, and the most striking feature of all.

The golden eyes were a feature unique to the Mists, and one rarely seen in the world anymore. The power they signified had resulted in a long history of enslavement for the species, and for many, the Mists were now little more than a myth.

Thick bands of gold, a symbol of that very enslavement, circled the wrists of the three now standing behind the Council, and hatred blazed in their eyes. Only a spell, controlled by the Council, prevented that gold from touching their skin and draining them of their magic and very life source.

The circumstances that led to the Mists being bound were a mystery to all but the Council. Darius knew only that it had resulted from the actions of Shayan, the youngest of the three. Stupidly, the male's sister, Maj, and older brother, Jannah, had sacrificed themselves to save him from death. *Idiots.*

After what seemed like an age, the Council broke apart and lowered their hoods. Kam indicated for the Mists to step forward, and they did so as if being forcefully dragged. A wave of power washed over the room, eliciting gasps from a number of Witnesses.

"By the terms of your servitude, we can only enforce your actions if all five of the Council are in agreement." Kam paused, looking at each of the Council members in turn. His gaze hesitated at Diana before finally resting on William. "That is not the case here today, so we must instead ask for your assistance."

Jannah, the oldest of the three, instantly stood taller, tension leaving his body. His answer was clear in the stubborn tilt of his chin.

Kam set out the Council's requirements and their reasoning: kill the hybrid and save the Lore.

Shayan tilted his head and assessed the Council. "You ask a lot from us. What will you give us in return?"

"We will let your sister go free." Vlad leered at the female.

Maj made to lunge for him, but he held up a finger and wagged it tauntingly. Jannah placed a hand on her shoulder and glared a warning at Shayan.

The young Mist ignored it.

"All of us. Let us all go and I'll do what you're too scared to do yourself." Shayan sneered and turned his back, arms crossed as he looked around the chamber, seemingly unimpressed with the proceedings.

"Shayan." Jannah's voice rumbled through the amphitheatre, causing every Supe in the room to shiver.

"And what if you fail?" Méabh sidled up to Shayan. She

walked a circle around him, trailing a fingernail across the broad expanse of his back. Her face was a mix of calculating assessment and carnal admiration as she brushed against him.

Shayan hesitated. He glanced at his brother and sister, then squared his shoulders and fixed his golden gaze on the fae.

"If I fail, I'll be yours to command. With no restrictions."

"No!" Maj pushed herself forward and placed herself between her younger brother and Méabh, mouth set in a resigned line. "If he fails, then I shall finish the job."

Shayan put a hand on her arm, golden eyes beseeching her. "I can do this, Maj. I can fix everything. Let me do this."

Méabh tapped the blood red nail against her lips and watched them quietly for a moment. "I don't know. I think I prefer his offer." She pointed to Shayan and smiled suggestively.

Before Maj could argue further, Jannah stepped forward, his fists clenched by his side.

"If he fails, we shall both ensure the job is finished. That is the only deal you'll get from us."

Méabh pouted her luscious red lips, then shrugged and walked back to the other Council members, giving Vlad a wink as she passed him.

The vampire ignored her, turning instead towards Diana. "We have our assassins. Now we need the witch. It's time for you to make yourself useful."

14

It's all gone.

Phoenix faced the charred and crumbling building that used to be her home and bit back the tears that burned her throat. Ethan stood by her side, an unwavering pillar of strength. But nothing could comfort her at that moment.

Abi had been silent since they arrived, and when she walked ahead of them, they hung back to give her some privacy. In truth, she couldn't bear to see the look of pain on her friend's face. The pub had been everything to Abi. It was the only thing she had left after her mother died, and now it was in ruins.

The heavy wooden door was little more than a pile of ash, allowing a glimpse of the devastation inside. Windows were gaping holes of jagged glass, and the roof had collapsed in a number of places. The general shape of the building had been maintained by the brickwork, but every-thing that had given it its character, its soul, had been destroyed.

It had taken her two days to gather the courage to come

back. She knew she had to see it for herself, but she couldn't face the truth of what she'd cost them. What she'd cost Abi. Eventually, her friend insisted she was well enough to go and Phoenix had no more excuses.

Ethan peered inside the doorway and let out a low whistle. "The witch's fire did all this damage?"

The memory of the explosion rang in her ears, and she shrugged. "The fire. The alcohol. Who knows?"

It didn't really matter how the pub was destroyed. She was the reason it had happened; the how was immaterial.

To her left, Abi peered through one of the shattered windows. When she saw the wreckage inside, she let out a sharp sob and sank to the ground with her hand over her mouth.

Phoenix ran to her side, ignoring the lance of pain as guilt speared her in the chest. She crouched down beside her friend and was surprised to see no tears on Abi's face. Her skin was still the sickly pale it had been since the fire, and rage blazed in her eyes, but no tears.

Abi grabbed her hand and gave it a tight squeeze, her mouth set in a determined line as she looked up at the carcass of her home and livelihood.

They sat together in silence for a few minutes, each lost in their own thoughts as they assessed the damage. Eventually, they stood and walked back to the main entrance where Ethan waited patiently.

"It's not safe for you to stay anymore. You know that."

His voice was gentle, but still the words caused her throat to tighten. She couldn't argue – not when the evidence was laid out so starkly before them – so she swallowed past the lump that choked her and nodded.

"What about Abi? She needs somewhere to go while ..." She looked at the damage before her, not even able to contemplate how it might be undone.

"I'm going with you."

Her jaw dropped, and she gaped at the obviously insane human beside her. When all she got in return was steely resolve, she turned to Ethan for support. A smile tugged at the corner of his mouth and he held up his hands, backing away from both of them.

What the hell? Has everyone lost their mind?

"Abi, I really don't think that's a good idea." She waved a hand towards the incinerated building, as if the obvious needed to be highlighted. "You could have died in that fire."

"Yep, and I could walk outside the door and get hit by a bus. I'm going with you, and you're going to train me to fight." Without waiting for a response, Abi turned and walked to Ethan's car, leaving Phoenix and Ethan staring after her in shock.

A low chuckle from Ethan was enough to redirect her irritation.

"Surely you can't think this is a good idea?" She planted her hands on her hips and glared at him.

"Of course not." He grew serious. "But it's her decision, and damned if I don't respect her for it. We'll protect her, Phoenix. She's already a target, whether you like it or not. Leaving her behind won't change that."

She sighed, wishing yet again that she could argue with him. And wasn't Abi the reason she refused to leave in the first place? One of the reasons, at least?

Needing a minute to gather her thoughts, she excused

herself and slipped into the wreckage of the pub. She had one more thing to do before they left.

The interior was a mess of ash and charred remains, yet there was a clear pattern to the destruction. She followed the path that ran from the entrance – or what remained of it – straight to the door that led to their apartment. There was a gaping hole where the bar had been and only small sections of the stage and seating area were intact, but the route the witch had taken was clearly marked by the lack of debris; as if the fire had burned everything clean away, even the dirt.

She only allowed herself a brief glance around before she forced her attention straight ahead and focused on her goal. There'd be time to grieve later.

The stairs leading to their apartment were barely standing. The skeleton structure remained, but sections of steps were missing and the ones that were left looked like they'd crumble under her weight. With a deep breath, she took them at a run, rebounding off the edges and crossing her fingers that she'd make it to the top before they collapsed entirely.

She did, just about.

Upstairs had fared a little better than the pub below, with the damage concentrated mainly around the hallway. The plasterboard walls on either side had burned away, and the rooms beyond were visible through gaping holes. Shafts of daylight shone down in the places where the roof was missing, and a chilling breeze filled the once cosy space.

She reached under her jacket to clasp the medallion that hung against her breastbone and hoped against hope.

The floors creaked in protest as she made her way to her bedroom with her breath held.

While the rest of the apartment looked to only have sustained fire damage, her room had obviously been the focus of some serious pent-up anger. The bed, alone, remained intact, and even that was half buried under a barely recognisable pile of rubble.

She rushed towards the heap of oak slabs that had once been her wardrobe, and a mix of terror and rage welled up inside her. Panic clawed at her throat, but she pushed it back with effort. She knelt and carefully began to move the pieces aside, one at a time.

When a patch of mahogany came into view, her head swam with relief. The knot of fear didn't unravel fully until she pulled the long box, miraculously intact, from the wreckage. Intricate Celtic symbols covered the wood, and her heart clenched at the familiar sight. She opened the box to reassure herself the sword was also unharmed, then quickly closed it and stood.

A niggling thought played at the back of her mind, and she cast her eyes to her bedside locker where she'd last seen the box for the Ritual of Passing. There was nothing there now besides ash, broken wood, and some stray herbs. A chilling sense of foreboding slithered down her spine as she turned and left the room.

15

The sharp wind bit at Lily's skin as she stood in front of the abandoned warehouse. She paid it little heed as she stared at the place where Annabelle had died. The industrial estate around her was silent, all the other businesses now closed for the night, but still she clutched her bag tight to her side. It wasn't the first time she'd found herself drawn to that exact spot, trying to imagine what her sister's last moments had been like.

Had she been afraid?

Had she called for her big sister?

It seemed odd that such an innocuous looking building could be the scene of something so tremendous, like the shattering of her world. Yet something lingered in the air. Death wasn't a stranger to this place.

She wasn't really sure what she hoped to achieve by coming here. Inspiration, maybe?

Through the cloth of her canvas bag, the heat of the Ouroboros called to her. Judging her. She could feel its power, but still it was out of reach. Despite the cold night air, her hands grew clammy. What if she wasn't strong enough? What if it was too late?

Someone cleared their throat softly behind her and she jumped. Lily pulled her magic to her, ready to strike as she turned to face the woman who'd appeared seemingly out of thin air.

A palpable sense of power surrounded the woman, and her signature was unmistakably that of a witch. She had a kind smile and long blonde hair similar to her own, but it was the green eyes that made Lily's heart clench; the compassion and wisdom behind them was so reminiscent of her mother that for a second, she was a child again and wanted nothing more than to be held in the safety of her mother's arms.

Lily shook herself and took a step back. The woman may be a witch, but that did not make her a friend. After all, it had been a witch that killed Annabelle. And their parents.

"Sorry, I didn't mean to startle you." The woman made no attempt to move closer, just watched her with those green eyes. "You're Lily, right?"

Lily tensed. *How does she know my name?*

"I'm Diana."

The name hung in the air between them and Lily's breath hitched. Diana? As in, the head of the witches?

"You're from the Council," she whispered, her heart hammering in her chest as her body's survival instinct suddenly realised how fucked she was.

Diana hesitated for a moment, then nodded. "We want to help you."

"That's very kind" – Lily cringed at the tremor in her voice – "but I'm not sure what you could help me with."

She took a small step to the left, watching closely for any reaction. A raised eyebrow directed at the canvas bag caused her to clutch it tighter as a new fear settled in the pit of her stomach.

Diana turned away from her to give the warehouse her full attention. "I knew your parents, you know. They were good witches, powerful. What happened to them was terrible, and it never should have happened." She sighed. "It must be hard for you to have lost them so young. And then your sister ... I can only imagine how painful it is, knowing you couldn't protect her."

The words sent a stabbing pain through Lily's heart. She raised her hand, half expecting to find a wound there, but there was nothing. Nothing other than her own guilt and the agony of the truth spoken aloud.

"I tried, I ... Annabelle was very strong-willed."

Diana gave her a sympathetic smile. "It's a trait of some of the best witches."

Lily's throat burned as she remembered the eagerness with which Annabelle had taken to her studies; even before she was old enough, she'd watch Lily and try to copy everything she was doing. She was determined to be a great witch, and no one was going to stop her.

"She would have been ... one of the best."

"She still can be." Diana turned to face her, the warehouse looming behind her. "We can help you use the Ouroboros."

A heavy weight pressed on Lily's chest, almost suffocating her as she tried to push it back. She knew better than to give in to the hope, knew better than to trust the Council. But what if …

"I'm not giving it to you."

"I'm not asking you to. The Council has plenty of magic at our disposal; we've no need for an old relic."

"Then what do you want from me?"

"Your help." Diana assessed her carefully. "There is only one way to stop the prophecy and save our people. The hybrid has to die."

She held up a hand to halt the protest that was on the tip of Lily's tongue. "You know I speak the truth. All we're asking from you is information. Keep us informed of the hybrid's whereabouts, and we can make sure no one else gets hurt. No one else has to die, Lily."

So many emotions rushed through Lily: fear, anger, guilt. It was Phoenix's fault this was all happening. If it hadn't been for her, the prophecy would never exist. Both Abi and Diana had now said this was the only way. But could she do it? Could she really give Phoenix up to the Council? Would she be able to look herself in the mirror again if she did? Would she be able to face her sister again?

And it was that thought that pulled her up short. The chance of seeing her sister again. She'd do anything to make that happen.

Even if it meant selling her soul.

16

The scenery all blurred into one as Phoenix rested her head against the car window. City turned to motorway, then to rolling green fields as far as the eye could see before starting the cycle all over again. Four hours they'd been driving only to end up in the Wicklow Mountains, barely an hour from where they'd first started. She hadn't argued when Ethan suggested it was worth leaving a false trail; she'd learned the hard way what it cost to take unnecessary risks.

Ethan was quiet in the driver's seat beside her. He threw the occasional sideways glance her way between watching the road ahead and flicking to the rear-view mirror, but overall he left her to her silent musings.

After the first hour, the hum of the rental car's engine had become soothing and lulled her into a mild sense of relaxation. It hadn't kept the niggling worries from flitting at the edge of her thoughts though, and every now and then, the relaxation would turn to a suffocating panic.

"Are you sure Abi will be safe with them?" she asked for the third time.

He spared her a reassuring smile despite the frustration he was no doubt feeling at answering the question yet again.

"Nate will watch out for her. The most dangerous place she can be right now is with you. It's better this way. At least until we know the trail is clear."

What he said made sense; hell, she'd even agreed to the plan. The others would lay low in a safe house in Galway while she and Ethan ran a diversion to draw out anyone that might follow them. Nate would use the time to try to hack deeper into the Council's network and find out what they were planning next. Then, once the coast was clear, they'd all regroup and head to Donegal together. That way they'd at least be limiting the trouble they were bringing with them.

Abi's response to the plan had been less agreeable; she refused point-blank to leave Phoenix's side. It had taken a lot of convincing, and a pinkie promise to check in every hour, before her friend had conceded. Nate's offer of self-defence training helped sweeten the deal too. Abi had been eager to learn, but the fact she needed to just made Phoenix feel worse.

Considering everything that had happened, it meant a lot that Abi was still so adamant about sticking by her. And that was why Phoenix knew this plan was the right one. If the Council was going to follow anyone, it would be her; she'd do everything in her power to lead that danger away from the others.

As the road sloped upward, the smooth tarmac was replaced with potholes and gravel. Trees lined the narrowing road and ditches awaited the unprepared. The 80 kph speed limit suddenly seemed a lot more question-able, even taking into account their so-called immortality.

They'd passed the last village fifteen minutes prior, and glimpses of civilisation had become fewer and farther between – a quaint bungalow here, the occasional farm there. Instead, sheep and cows dotted the lush green fields and breaks in the treeline afforded unobstructed views of breath-taking valleys and forests.

Her chest constricted as she remembered the last time she'd been in these mountains. Ten years ago, she'd walked out of her family home. She'd never found the strength to come back. Not until now.

As if reading her thoughts, Ethan asked softly, "Do you want to go see the house?"

She bit her lip hard and shook her head.

He reached out and gave her hand a quick squeeze before returning his focus to the road, an unreadable expression on his face.

They drove for another few minutes in silence before Ethan pulled the car to a stop in front of a small pub that appeared seemingly out of nowhere. A thatched roof and white pebble-dashed walls gave the building a quaint feel, but the blue wooden door and window frames were weath-ered and in need of a lick of paint. A B&B sign hung beside the door, creaking as it swung gently in the breeze.

Phoenix hesitated before getting out of the car. So, this was their first stop? The place seemed so normal. A whisper of anxiety bubbled up in her throat as she imagined what magic fire could do to the thatched roof.

She trailed behind Ethan as he headed into the pub. Darkness shrouded them as the light of the sun gave way to shadowy nooks and crannies filled with wood and exposed stonework. The smell of freshly poured Guinness reached her nose and her chest ached at the thought of home. Then she noticed the silence.

A glance around the room confirmed that all eyes were on them. She squirmed under their scrutiny.

Two men in jeans and checked shirts sat on high stools at the bar with cold pints resting in weathered hands. A middle-aged couple sat in one corner, an unlit stone fireplace forming their backdrop. And an old man occupied the opposite corner, a newspaper in one hand, pint in the other. All were watching the newcomers with a mix of curiosity and suspicion, and Phoenix suddenly understood what it felt like to be an animal in the zoo.

Unperturbed, Ethan grabbed her hand and plastered a friendly smile on his face as he pulled her to the bar.

"Just a minute. Just a minute," came a woman's voice from a doorway to the rear.

Phoenix raised her eyebrows at Ethan, but he said nothing, just leaned against the bar, looking as relaxed as always.

A couple of very silent, very uncomfortable minutes later, a woman came bustling from the back room, looking somewhat dishevelled as she wiped her hands on a tea towel. Her mousy brown hair was pulled back in a messy knot and her black top was covered in flour, but her smile was friendly, and she wore the lines on her face comfortably.

"Now, what can I get you, folk?"

Ethan's smile grew wider. "A Malibu and coke for the lady, and a pint of your finest for me. Also, would you happen to have a room for the night?"

The woman eyed them both for a minute, her gaze flicking to Phoenix's left hand resting on the bar.

Phoenix's cheeks grew hot as she realised the conclusions the woman was no doubt jumping to, and she shoved the hand self-consciously into her pocket.

Assessment done, the woman nodded and began to prepare the drinks. "Room is eighty a night, breakfast included. Pub closes at eleven, so no loud music after that. Local church is back in the village and holds a six o'clock service. Band sets up at eight to give everyone time to get back from mass." The woman placed their drinks on the bar in front of them and smiled. "Oh, and I'm Maura."

Phoenix took a welcome sip of her drink while Ethan handed over some money and received a room key in return. A low murmur of conversation had returned to the pub, but she could still feel the stares burning into the back of her head, and it was obvious the conversations were only half-hearted attempts to cover the eavesdropping.

When he was done, Ethan nodded back towards the door and, with a smile of thanks to Maura, they took their drinks and headed for one of the empty picnic tables outside.

"Jeez," she said, once they were seated out of earshot. "That was about as comfortable as an anal probe."

Ethan snorted, choking on the first gulp of his pint. "I

wouldn't know. Besides, you grew up not too far from here. You should be well used to the local welcome."

A huff was all she gave him in reply.

They sat in silence, watching as the sun sank lower on the horizon and the air turned chilly. Ethan glanced sideways at her. "You look tired."

She shrugged. Sleep wasn't coming too easy right now, and she'd spent the past few nights tossing and turning in Ethan's spare room. When she did finally fall asleep, her dreams went on a never-ending loop involving a gaping black hole and her dying in the most horrendous ways possible.

Last night's dream had been the worst; all she remembered were the cries for help before waking in a pool of sweat. It had taken her a long time to rid her mind of the sound and shake the feeling that there was someone she needed to save.

Ethan stood and offered her a hand. "Why don't we check out the room? You can catch a quick nap before we use you as bait."

Ethan unlocked the door to the B&B room and moved aside to let Phoenix pass. He followed her in and his eyes fell on the double bed that occupied most of the space. The floral bed covers were a complete eyesore and reminded him of something from the eighties. The room was clean though, and a matching floral armchair sat by the large picture window, affording a breath–taking view of the hills.

Phoenix came to an abrupt halt beside him as she, too,

noticed the lone bed. She tensed and started tugging nervously at her sleeve.

Something tightened inside him, and he clenched his jaw as irritation mixed with something that felt a little like hurt.

"Don't get your knickers in a twist." He stepped past her towards the bathroom. "I'll take the floor."

He closed the bathroom door a little harder than necessary and leaned back against it. Was the thought of sharing a room with him really that bad? It wasn't like he was going to ravage her while she slept. Hell, it was the twenty-first century; she should be the one taking the floor.

With a weary sigh, he went to the avocado-coloured sink and splashed cold water over his face. Phoenix would just have to suck it up because he wasn't leaving her alone again. His wolf growled in agreement; she was theirs to protect.

What part of him had thought being alone with her would be simple? Just being near her drove him crazy. He'd basically signed himself up for a week of torture.

Ever since their kiss in Darius's lair, he'd gone out of his way to give her space. After the role he'd played in her parents' sacrifice, he had no right to push her. Some stupid part of him had actually hoped she'd come to him of her own choice if he just gave her time. Instead, her walls had gone straight back up, and the glimmer of passion she'd allowed him to see haunted his dreams.

Maybe it was time they laid it all out on the table once and for all. A straight up conversation with no bullshit. Grabbing a towel from the radiator, he dried his face, decision made. Before he could second-guess himself, he yanked open the bathroom door. And stopped.

Phoenix lay on the garish bed covers, her breathing soft, in sync with the gentle rise and fall of her chest. Her eyes were closed, and for once, the tension was absent from her face.

He leaned his head against the doorframe and sighed.

17

Darius absently swirled the golden liquid around the crystal tumbler as he stared out the viewing window of his club. Even at this height, the scent of blood reached him and his fangs ached for something with a bit more bite than the smooth whiskey. But it would have to wait; business first, pleasure later.

The door opened behind him and he pressed a button on the wall to turn the glass black. He knocked back the whiskey and turned to face the wolf that eyed him warily from the doorway.

"Sit," he ordered, indicating towards the velvet sofa.

There was a slight hesitation before the man complied. Blue eyes tracked his every movement as he picked up a file from his desk and placed it on the table between them. He opened the file and fanned out the security footage images so that each was clearly visible.

The flinch was subtle but enough to catch his attention.

"Tell me, Omega, do you recognise anyone in this image?" He pointed to a still taken from the security cameras in the Dublin lair, almost a month prior. The picture showed Phoenix leaving the lair with a number of others in tow. One of which he knew to be a wolf.

Silence was the only answer that came, and the wolf held his face in a blank mask, obscured by the tangled white hair that fell in front of his eyes. The flinch had been enough, however.

"Need I remind you that you only remain alive so long as you're useful to me?" Darius let the warning hang in the air between them before twisting the knife in fully. "What do you think will happen to the other wolves if you're gone?"

Blue eyes tightened in pain, and he knew the wolf would answer. The Omega's nature had proven key in helping Darius to control the temperament of his test wolves. That very same nature would make it impossible for the man to turn his back on the other wolves, not if it would cause them pain.

"The wolf's name is Ethan," the Omega ground out eventually, each syllable torn reluctantly from his mouth.

Darius raised an eyebrow. "How is it you happen to know his name?"

The man clenched his fists and his whole body shook as he warred with himself.

"He is the son of my pack Alpha."

Now that was interesting. He'd hoped to use the Omega to track Phoenix and maybe find out some information about her associates since they'd been such a thorn in his side. But this was an unexpected bonus.

"Your *old* pack, where was it based?"

A bead of sweat ran down the Omega's forehead and his

knuckles turned white from clenching so hard, but still he answered.

"Donegal."

"Would he go there? Would his pack help him protect someone not of their species?"

"Cormac would do anything for his son."

"Even defy the Council?"

A small smile twitched at the corner of the Omega's mouth. "If it gave him a chance to defy his cousin? Most definitely."

Darius stilled. "His cousin?"

"Cormac's cousin, William, is the head of the werewolves."

18

Confusion clouded Phoenix's mind as she climbed her way back to consciousness. The room around her was dark, and her heart pounded as she tried to place the strange-smelling sheets and the too-soft mattress. It took a moment for the fog to lift enough to remember where she was.

Flustered, she sat up. The bed covers were rumpled beneath her and a thin line of drool ran down her chin. How long had she been asleep for?

The sound of running water filtered into her conscious-ness and she looked around, realising she was alone in the room. An image of Ethan in the shower flashed unbidden into her head.

She pushed the thought from her mind and grabbed the backpack Ethan had left at the side of the bed for her. A quick rummage through it for her phone somehow produced a hairbrush. She looked at it in disgust, but then her gaze flicked towards the bathroom door. Shaking her head, she yanked the brush through her hair, then shoved it back into the bag. She was pathetic.

The next rummage actually produced her phone, and she pressed speed dial on Abi's number before she was overtaken by some other stupid urge, like putting make-up on.

"Fifi! Thank god. I've been so worried. Did you get there okay? Ethan's not leaving you alone, is he?"

Her mind once more flashed to the thought of Ethan naked and suddy in the shower. She had to clear her throat before answering. "Nope, he's not giving me an inch. Sorry I didn't call sooner. We got here a few hours ago, but I fell asleep. Guess I was more tired than I realised. You're at the safe house, right?"

She listened as Abi babbled excitedly about their hideout in Galway and the self-defence training Nate had dutifully started with her. He'd declared her a natural after she caught him with an unexpected knee to the balls.

"Supe or not, it works on them all," Abi proclaimed proudly.

Phoenix's laughter died in her throat as the bathroom door opened and Ethan walked into the room with his jeans slung low on his hips and bare chest still damp. The serious look on his face morphed into a cheeky grin when he caught her staring. She turned her back, cheeks burning.

"What? ... Yeah, I'm listening," she blustered, suddenly realising that Abi had continued talking. "Look, I gotta go. Promise me you'll be careful, okay?"

Even after Abi hung up, she waited until Ethan cleared his throat before turning back around. He'd taken the time to put on a t-shirt, but the twinkle in his eyes was still present.

"Like what you –" He was stopped from finishing his question by the ping of his phone.

A quick glance at the screen and all signs of teasing fell from his face. Something that looked worryingly like fear flitted over his features before his jaw settled in a hard line and he shoved the phone into his pocket.

"Ethan?"

He was quiet for a moment before looking at her with serious brown eyes. "We've got trouble. Let's go. I'll explain while we check out the area." He didn't wait for her to respond, just grabbed his jacket and headed out the door.

She grumbled to herself about annoying werewolves, but plucked her leather jacket from the end of the bed and followed him, closing the door behind her.

They made their way through the hallway of the B&B to the bar where a band was busy setting up in the corner. The locals, fresh from evening mass, once more turned their microscopes to examine the newcomers in their midst. She kept her head down and tried to ignore the curious stares as she trailed Ethan to the front of the pub. They'd just reached the door when Maura appeared from nowhere with a tray of drinks in hand.

"All settled in?" She wiggled her eyebrows with a mischievous glint in her eyes that caused Phoenix's cheeks to burn again. "You're just in time. The band should be starting shortly."

Ethan returned her smile with a charming grin as he placed a warm hand on the small of Phoenix's back. The heat of his touch seared through her clothes.

"We were actually just going to take a stroll, have a look around the area."

The smile fell from Maura's face and her forehead creased with concern. "I'm not sure it's a good idea for you to go wandering at this time of the evening."

There was an awkward pause as the landlady hesitated. With a conspiratorial glance around her, she leaned in and lowered her voice. "The fairies have been up to no good lately. It's really not safe out there at night."

Phoenix choked in surprise and bit the inside of her cheek in an attempt at keeping a straight face. Mirth sparkled in Ethan's eyes as he patted her back.

"Oh really? What have they been up to?" he asked, the picture of innocent concern.

"Well, there's been a lot of animals killed. And then there's them freak storms. Now I'm not saying the fair folk can control the weather or anything but ..." She gave them a knowing look.

Ethan raised an eyebrow. "What makes you so sure the fairies are responsible? Maybe there's a wild animal on the loose?"

Maura clucked her tongue and shook her head adamantly. "Ain't no wild animal doing this. Not with the way these animals are being killed. I always said that fairy ring up the hill would bring trouble. John – Lord rest his soul – said I was off my rocker, but I knew."

Before either of them could respond, a shout from across the bar grabbed Maura's attention and, with a smile, she hurried off.

Phoenix looked after her in disbelief as Ethan chuckled beside her.

"Fancy checking out a real live fairy ring?"

Night had coated the area in a blanket of darkness, broken only by the map of stars twinkling above them and a sliver of the moon. This far from any villages or towns, there was very little artificial light to guide them along the gravelly path that doubled as a highly suspect road. Phoenix shivered as she cast her eyes around at the hedges and forests that provided more hiding places than she was comfortable with.

"So, what trouble are we in now?"

She was suddenly conscious of the metaphorical target pinned to her back, and their earlier plan didn't seem quite so clever. Why the hell had she agreed to be bait? Sure, it would help draw out anyone who might be following them, but it also had the potential side-effect of death.

"They're sending the Mists."

Ethan's words broke through her rambling thoughts and she stumbled to a stop. "What?"

He turned to look at her, running a hand through his hair. "Dad texted. The Council is sending the Mists."

She opened her mouth and closed it again. Like every other Supe in existence, she'd grown up with horror stories about the Mists – tales of the bogeyman that were meant to keep young, powerful, unpredictable children in line. She'd never really thought ...

"So, they're real?"

His jaw clenched tight as he nodded. "Phoenix, I don't know if I can protect –"

He stilled.

Adrenaline shot through her veins at the sudden

tension radiating from him. She strained but couldn't hear anything aside from the soft rustle of leaves and whistle of wind through the trees.

Ethan grabbed her hand, motioned for her to stay silent. He pulled her through a small gap in the hedges into the empty field beside them, urging her to keep low as he beckoned her to follow him along the thorny brambles.

With the wind at their backs, it took her senses a little longer to catch up to his wolf ones, but soon the stench of decay hit her and she knew instantly what had put Ethan on high alert.

At the peak of the hill, they reached a small farm. Sheep and cows huddled together at the far end of the field, little more than dark blobs as their nervous bleating created an anxious symphony in the otherwise silent night. The pen that should have contained them was broken in places, the fences trampled and useless in restraining its occupants. It was from there that the stench emanated. She forced herself to take shallow breaths through her mouth as they drew closer.

The sight in front of them caused her stomach to heave and tears to prick her eyes. It was impossible to count how many lambs lay mauled in the grass with blood staining their once pristine coats. Insides trailed outside, and despite Maura's earlier words, Phoenix's first thought was animal attack.

Ethan crouched down beside one of the lambs for a closer look, and when he turned back to her, his face was puzzled. "These bites are from human teeth."

"What?"

Distracted enough by his comment to block out the

gore for a moment, she moved to his side for a closer look. Sure enough, she could make out marks roughly the size of a human bite circumference, and damage that was clearly done by blunt teeth rather than the fangs of an animal.

"Don't get me wrong" – she swallowed back the bile that rose in her throat – "I'm no vegetarian, but that's just gross."

He gave her a wry smile and stood, nodding towards the small farmhouse in the distance. "I think we should probably go check on the owners. It's hard to tell with so much decay nearby, but we might have a few more surprises before the night's out."

She followed him with a resigned sigh, her eyes scanning the darkness for any movement. There were no lights on in the house, but a battered SUV sat in the drive and she saw no obvious sign of intrusion from the outside. Maybe whatever got the animals was full and left? Or maybe the Council had already sent the Mists and this was all a trap.

Ethan tried the door and it opened with a creak. The stench of death hit them like a furnace of hot air. Her stomach lurched and threatened to evict its contents, and she wanted nothing more than to turn and walk away.

Darkness filled the hallway, and the only sound was a low buzzing noise that seemed to come from the room at the far end. Ethan drew his hunting knife from inside his jacket and motioned for her to stay behind him.

Tentatively, they inched their way down the hall, pausing at each open doorway to check the rooms beyond. The further they moved into the house, the stronger the smell became, cloying at the back of her throat and making it hard to swallow.

The door at the end led to a small kitchen. Faded flower wallpaper covered the walls and a well-used stove sat nestled between oak cabinets. A wooden table filled the centre of the room, one chair occupied and the air around it swarming with flies.

"What the –"

The words left her mouth on a whispered breath, and the look she received from Ethan mirrored her own horror. She squinted as her brain struggled to make out what she was seeing.

The form definitely appeared human, or at least something of a similar shape. But beyond that, the features were almost indiscernible. A thick layer of grey sludge coated the body. It clung in parts, forming dips and troughs that may or may not have been eye sockets and a gaping mouth. And in others, it oozed, as if it were a living organism.

A floorboard creaked overhead and she froze. Her heart tripled its rhythm. She really did not want to meet whatever was responsible for this. This was a whole new level of fucked up.

Ethan, however, didn't seem to have the same reservations, and instead of moving towards the door like a sane person would, he motioned for her to follow him as he slipped back into the hall and made his way to the stairs.

She glared at his back even as her body stupidly followed. If he got her turned into a slimy corpse, she was so going to come back and haunt him.

Soft moonlight filtered in from a window at the top of the stairs, but it did little more than add an eerie backdrop to the horror movie they were so willingly traipsing into. All except one door on the upper level stood open, and she could hear a low scratching sound coming from inside. Her skin crawled and she shuddered.

Silently, they moved to the door, side by side. She held her breath and mentally cursed him for dragging her up here. He reached for the handle, met her eyes for a second, then pushed the door open.

Nothing.

The scratching continued, but nothing came barrelling out of the room to attack them. One breath. Two breaths. She looked at Ethan. He looked at her.

Her heart hammered in her chest as she slid down to a crouch and peered around the wooden frame of the door. Her jaw dropped.

The room was an explosion of 1980s floral and impeccably tidy. None of that was what caught her attention, however.

An old lady was hunkered down on the floor. Her body was in a position Phoenix wouldn't have thought possible given the fact she looked to easily be in her eighties. Her grey hair was wild around her head, and the white night-gown she wore was covered in dirt and blood.

She watched with a disturbed sense of detachment as the woman scratched words into the floral wallpaper with her fingernail. She'd obviously been doing it for quite some time as blood ran in rivulets from her fingers. When she was done, the words "THEY'RE COMING" were smeared across the wall in jagged letters.

Slowly, the woman's head turned in their direction, red eyes pulsing as she tilted her head at an unnatural angle to regard them.

"Shit," Ethan muttered under his breath.

Phoenix couldn't help but agree. The Council, Mists, and now this? Surely they shouldn't have to worry about demons on top of everything else.

For a moment, everyone stood still, assessing each other. The old lady eyed them like she'd just found her next meal. Then, with a hiss that showcased rotten black teeth, the demon lunged.

Ethan met the frail body in a clash that should have caused it to crumble. Instead, the demon's essence infused it with a speed and strength that beggared belief, and the old woman easily countered his attack.

Phoenix flung herself onto the demon's back in an attempt to slow it down, but a layer of slime seeped out from the woman's pores and her hands slipped off, unable to gain purchase.

Rotten teeth snapped at her face before Ethan grabbed the demon and flung it against the wall.

"Tell me you have an amulet with you?" He grunted as the demon rebounded and threw itself at him once more.

She fumbled in her pocket for the amulet she'd tucked away, but the slime coating her hands caused it to slip from her grasp and clatter to the floor. With a curse, she lunged to grab it, the sounds of fighting a ticking time bomb to her ears. In her panic, she sent it skittering under the bed.

Before she could reach for it, a strangled noise drew her attention upward. The demon had Ethan by the throat and appeared ready to eat his face off. Ethan's face turned puce as he struggled against the vice-like grip that was crushing his windpipe.

A glint of metal caught her eye and she spotted Ethan's

hunting knife on the ground a couple of feet from her. She grabbed it and flung it at the demon.

The blade lodged in the old woman's eye, and she let an inhuman screech that caused the windows, and Phoenix's bones, to rattle. With a final shrieking roar in their direction, the demon took a running leap and crashed through the first-floor window.

Phoenix reached for the broken glass at the same time as Ethan. Her resounding "Fuck!" was echoed by his own as they looked out into the empty night beyond.

Lily gritted her teeth and tried to sidestep Nate. At the far end of the safe house training studio, she could hear Abi on the phone, but she couldn't make out what was being said because he wouldn't shut the hell up.

"I'm worried about you. I know it's been hard for you since –" Nate prattled on as she tried in vain to block him out.

Was Abi frowning? Had something happened? She craned her neck, but Nate moved with her, blocking her eye-line again. She hadn't given Diana the location yet, so the Council couldn't have gotten to Phoenix already. Could Ethan have found out that they contacted her? Was Abi going to turn around any minute now and point an accusing finger in her direction?

"I just wanted you to know that I'm here if you need to talk or anything –"

What if they'd found Phoenix? What if they'd found another source and didn't need her anymore? Her heart stopped cold.

If they didn't need her, they'd have no reason to help her. At that thought, her chest tightened and she grew lightheaded, each breath she took seeming void of oxygen.

Beside her, Nate sighed in resignation. "I'll leave you alone."

She turned in a daze towards him and a distant part of her noted the deep sadness in his amber eyes; she'd never seen that look on his face before.

When she didn't say anything in return, he gave her a small smile and headed for the changing room behind them.

Guilt twisted her gut, and she opened her mouth to call him back and apologise. But she closed it just as quickly. There was nothing she could say to make him understand. Nothing that wouldn't make him hate her, at least.

At that moment, Abi hung up the phone and Lily's concerns about Nate's feelings were forgotten. She made a beeline in Abi's direction, only for Shade to step out in front of her before she got across the room.

She bit back a scream of frustration and met his intense blue gaze. "What?"

His scowl deepened. "Don't push your friends away, Lily."

His words made her bristle, but she held her tongue. With a defiant glare, she shoved past him and hurried to Abi's side. "Is everything okay?"

Abi nodded and gave her a small smile that didn't quite reach her eyes. "It appears Phoenix and Ethan have run into a slight demon problem. It got away and they've been out all night trying to track it down."

Lily's knees went weak with relief. Just a demon, not the Council. They still needed her.

"What are they going to do about it?"

"She said they're going to stick around another day to try to track it." Abi chewed her lip and looked at the blank screen of her phone. "Is that safe? Should they not keep moving in case the Council find them? Phoenix played it down when I asked, but I could tell she was worried."

Lily rubbed the girl's arm absently, her mind busy assessing how that affected her own plan. "I'm sure Ethan knows what he's doing."

Shade let out a low grunt from behind her, making her jump. "Yeah 'cause he always thinks clearly when he's around her." He turned and stalked towards the changing room.

Abi raised an eyebrow and looked at her. "I don't mean to overstep the mark or anything, but what's his deal?"

Lily stared in the direction of the changing rooms, something about the vampire's strange mood making her uneasy. "Shade doesn't exactly like Phoenix."

"He blames her for the prophecy."

She flicked her eyes back to Abi. "I guess so."

The other girl chewed that over for a few moments before excusing herself with a frown.

Lily watched her go and let out a shuddering breath. Her hands were shaking from the adrenaline thrumming through her veins, and she couldn't shake that terrifying thought of "what if".

The longer she waited, the more chance they'd find another way. She couldn't let that happen.

She squared her shoulders, and with renewed purpose,

made her way through the winding corridors of the safe house until she came to a door that would lead her outside. The cold air hit her like a slap, and dark clouds threatened rain as she stumbled her way through the vast grounds that surrounded the property.

Once she was far enough from prying eyes and ears, she pulled her phone out and pressed the call button. "Diana, it's Lily."

20

Phoenix hung her head and let the water from the shower pound across her shoulder blades until it turned cold and she was forced to step away from the soothing stream or face hypothermia. Shivering, she grabbed the nearby towel and wrapped it around herself. Steam fogged the small bathroom and she breathed deeply, letting the residual heat flow through her lungs.

After almost twelve hours straight searching the area, they still hadn't managed to find the demon, and she was starting to grow antsy. They couldn't just leave the locals at the mercy of a rampant slime monster, but how long would it take for the Council to find them? And if they were really sending the Mists ... Well, that didn't even bear thinking about.

When Ethan had suggested they get some rest before one last-ditch search, she'd agreed wearily. One more night, then they had to leave; demon or no demon.

With a sigh, she grabbed her clothes from the radiator and started dressing. She had her trousers half on when she heard Ethan's voice on the other side of the door. He was speaking quietly, but the agitation was evident in his tone. Balancing precariously with one leg in and one leg out of her trousers, she paused to listen.

"What does it matter if he knows? ... Of course I didn't contact him ... When? ... TONIGHT?"

She didn't have a chance to react to Ethan's roar before the bathroom door was flung open to reveal the werewolf with his phone pressed to his ear. He barely even blinked at her state of undress, simply ordered, "We need to go," before slamming the bathroom door closed.

Not quite sure what had happened, she gaped after him. An unreasonable voice in the back of her head mumbled that a little acknowledgement of her nakedness wouldn't go amiss as she shoved her foot through the other leg of her jeans.

When she emerged from the bathroom minutes later, she found him pacing the room, his hands clenching and unclenching as he stared at the door. Before she could even ask what was going on, he yanked open the door and waved for her to follow.

She raced to catch up with him, giving Maura a quick wave as they hurried through the pub and out into the night.

"Dammit, Ethan, what the hell is up?"

"We need to find the demon and get out of here. Now."

She came to an abrupt halt, her blood running cold. "What happened?"

He stopped and shoved his unruly hair back out of his face as he turned to her. "They've sent the first Mist."

"Oh."

Well, that sure took the wind out of her sails.

Ethan, too, seemed to deflate a little before her as he nodded. "Yeah, big oh. Somehow William found out about my connection to you. He sent my dad a warning out of courtesy. He said he can't protect me if I insist on being stupid."

She blew out a breath and watched it fog in the air in front of her. "Guess we need to get hunting."

With time working against them, they started up the hill again in search of their demon. Maura had told them at lunch that there'd been even more animals killed the night before. In a hushed voice she'd informed them that the farm owners, Seamus and Betty, had obviously annoyed the fair folk since the trail of dead animals led straight from their farm to the fairy ring.

Despite how ludicrous her logic was, Phoenix and Ethan both agreed it was as good a place as any to start their search. With any luck, they'd pick up a scent Ethan could follow.

"Your uncle didn't, by any chance, give you some idea how you might survive one of these Mists?"

Ethan grimaced. "You don't survive the Mists. You run."

Ah, just the cheery answer she was hoping for.

She opened her mouth to ask her next question – how long do you keep running for? – but he suddenly tensed and pulled up short.

Really? Again? Please let it be the bloody demon, at least.

She stood completely still and watched as Ethan tilted his head, jaw clenched in concentration.

"How sure are you that the ring forts are just a superstition?" he asked, voice barely a whisper.

She raised her eyebrows and swivelled her head to survey their surroundings. They'd nearly reached the peak of the hill, and the border of trees on either side were thinning out enough that she could see an open field on the far side, bathed in moonlight.

"What kind of stupid question is that?"

She shuddered at the creeping sensation that was working its way up from the base of her spine. Humans had bizarre imaginations; what relevance could a random circle in a field have to the fae?

"Can't you feel it?"

She shook her head, but a whisper of something tingled across the back of her neck. Subtle. Easily missed.

"There's magic of some kind here." Ethan's eyes searched their surroundings warily.

"The demon?" she suggested. But she already knew the answer. This didn't feel like the demon's energy; it was lacking the taint of evil.

Instead of answering, Ethan crouched low and stepped through a break in the trees into the field on the other side. She followed his lead, keeping her eyes peeled as they moved towards the raised hill of grass that formed the ring fort.

Unease tap-danced along her spine, and the feeling was immediately justified when a shadowy form came into view.

A body lay in the middle of the ring fort, spreadeagled and unmoving. The layer of clear slime that coated it glistened under the light of the moon and made her want another shower.

"Is that –"

"The farmer's wife." Ethan took a step closer, careful to stay out of reach.

"It found another host?" She searched the darkness, fully expecting the demon to emerge from the shadows at any second.

"Not quite," came a voice as smooth as silk in response.

21

The air shimmered before Phoenix's eyes, and she stepped into a defensive stance. Ethan shifted his position so that his back was to hers with his claws extended. Shadows entwined and coalesced, teasing a possible source for the voice, only to disappear and reappear in another location.

"Shit." Her heart hammered in her ears.

Ethan growled low in response.

"I thought you'd be grateful that I took care of your demon problem." The voice came again, brushing past her ear in a whisper.

Her body tensed instinctively at the touch. She forced her breathing to slow and waited. The shadows swirled in front of her, turning into a black smoke as a form began to solidify. The first thing that struck her were the golden eyes. The next was the heart-stopping smile.

Should my murderer look that charming? she wondered in a daze.

The glint of a silver sabre broke whatever spell held her mesmerised and she dived to the side, pulling Ethan with her. The blade sliced so close to her face that she closed her eyes to brace for the pain. When it didn't come, she leapt to her feet and looked at Ethan in a panic.

"How do we fight him?" she repeated her earlier question.

"We don't." He grabbed her hand. "We run."

He pulled so hard she nearly fell over. She stumbled to get her footing and followed him to the forest in the distance.

How fast were the Mists? Goddammit, why hadn't she asked more bloody questions when she had the chance?

Somehow, they reached the trees. Branches scraped her arms and face as she pushed through the dense copse. Shadows moved around her, and the night seemed alive with strange noises that filled her head and caused her sense of direction to become disorientated.

Her vision blurred, but still she kept running, forcing her instincts to focus only on Ethan's energy ahead of her.

"Run all you want," the silky voice whispered in her ear. "You're just making it harder on yourself."

The tree in front of her burst into flame and she was forced to veer sharply to the left.

Shit. Where's Ethan?

The Mist's laughter followed her, but the shadows were no longer lapping at her heels. Instead, they swirled leisurely through the trees, weaving a trail of fire that would soon box her in.

"Ethan," she yelled, frantically searching the thick block of trees around her.

"He can't help you now," came the reply at her back.

She turned just in time to see a rueful smile on the

charming face of death as the Mist reached a glowing gold fist towards her.

A loud growl was the only indication she had of Ethan's whereabouts before a large brown wolf leapt between her and the Mist. The golden fist plunged through the wolf's chest, and she watched in horror as its whole body went rigid and Ethan's now yellow eyes widened in shock.

"No!" she screamed, wrapping her arms tightly around the rough fur, as if that alone could stop the fist from crushing his heart.

Heat built in her chest as fear for Ethan overwhelmed her. She clenched her eyes closed and gave herself over to the magic. They were dead either way.

With her chest pressed close to the wolf's body, she could feel when his heart began to slow. She let all of the fear, all of the anger fill her, and in a flash of blinding white light, she let it go.

Once more, the night went black.

Daylight flared through Phoenix's eyelids and pain exploded in her head. She scrunched her eyes tight against the glare. The ground beneath her was hard and unyielding, and every part of her ached.

Shit. Her eyes flew open and heart leapt into her throat. Where was she?

Scorched earth filled her immediate eye-line and gnarled trees loomed over her, their barks blackened. She kept completely still even as her heart thundered in her chest.

Was he still here? The Mist. Was he waiting for her to wake so he could kill her?

When minutes passed with no sound other than her soft breathing, she glanced carefully around. She was lying in a small clearing surrounded on all sides by trees. The ground under her was little more than charred dirt, devoid of the lush vegetation that covered the rest of the forest. A large lump of brown fur lay at her feet, unmoving. She saw the wolf, but it took her brain a minute to connect the dots.

Ethan!

She scrambled to her knees, the memories flooding back: golden eyes, a glowing fist, the all-consuming heat of the sun. Her hands trembled as she ran them over the coarse fur, searching for injuries. *Please be okay. Please be okay.*

He was still alive. She knew because she could hear the sluggish beat of his heart as it laboured to pump blood around his body. But his breathing was shallow, and he showed no reaction to her touch. There were no burns that she could see. How was that? She was holding him when the sun's power had exploded from her. He should be dead. They both should be.

A light breeze blew through the trees, rustling the leaves, and her heart pounded. She looked around, suddenly aware of the ominous shadows that lurked between the trees.

What happened to the Mist when she called the sun? Did it kill him, or was he hiding in one of those shadows? A cold sweat broke out on the back of her neck. They needed to get the hell out of here.

She climbed to her feet, and with extreme effort,

manoeuvred the huge wolf so that she could hoist it over her shoulder. Even with supernatural strength, the weight knocked the wind out of her.

There was no stealth to her trek back to the B&B, and she could only hope none of the locals saw her or the giant "dog" she was carrying. It was very possible Ethan sustained some bumps to the head along the way, but she figured it'd do him no harm – maybe even knock some sense into him. If he ever woke up…

The sun was cresting the horizon as she reached the pub and miraculously made it to their room. She lay Ethan on the bed and slumped down beside him, gently running her fingers through the fur at the nape of his neck.

Why hadn't he changed back? Or regained consciousness? His body should be healing any damage. She bit her lip.

On the locker beside her, red numbers flashed on the small alarm clock. A taunting reminder that they were on borrowed time. The Mist would be back. She didn't know what had happened after the world went black, but her gut was telling her he was alive. They couldn't afford to be here when he returned.

Five more minutes, she decided, staring at the blinking numbers. She'd rest for five minutes, and then they had to leave.

She set about packing their meagre belongings, wrote a brief note of thanks to Maura, and looked back to the clock, resigned to her fate. Time to go.

Getting an unconscious werewolf to the car unnoticed was another feat she hadn't expected to manage, but it seemed someone up there was taking pity on her. She slid behind the wheel of their car, Ethan resting across the back seat, still in wolf form. Her gaze flicked from him to the small pub, and an icy thread of fear slid through her as she hoped like hell they weren't leaving a trail of destruction in their wake.

22

There was complete silence in the chamber as Shayan kneeled before the Council. Deep burns marred his handsome features, vivid red blending into blackened patches of skin. Even from where Darius stood at the edge of the crowd, he could see the defiance blazing in those golden eyes and he shook his head; the boy had a death wish.

His focus at that moment wasn't the Mist, however, but rather the Council. More specifically, William.

The blood red cloak covering the werewolf didn't quite conceal the fists clenched at his side, and there was a tightness to his jaw that was perceptible only because Darius was looking so closely.

He'd seen that same tic the evening before when he'd innocently approached William as a concerned Witness. Of course, the reaction had been preceded by barely concealed shock when Darius mentioned rumours of a particular werewolf being involved with the hybrid.

"I can't imagine it was easy for you," he'd declared

solemnly. "To send the Mist knowing it would put your own blood in danger."

The flinch had been subtle and just what Darius had hoped for. He needed Phoenix alive at all costs, which meant he needed to exploit any weak link he could find.

"I appreciate your concern, Witness," William had growled, "but the Council will do what needs to be done. The first Mist is being dispatched as we speak."

Needless to say, that wasn't the news Darius had been hoping for. He'd contacted his head of security immediately with an instruction to find Phoenix or face the final death. They'd managed to locate her, but by that stage it was dawn and the Witnesses had already been summoned for an update.

"Tell us again what happened," William ordered Shayan, his voice a low rumble filled with warning.

As the Mist once more relayed his encounter, Darius couldn't help the smirk of satisfaction that lifted the corner of his mouth. Despite all the odds, Phoenix seemed, yet again, to survive on pure blind luck. And to hear that a werewolf got injured during the fight, well, that was just unfortunate.

"I'll finish the job. Just get me the next location." Shayan rose to his feet and faced the Council with his chin held high and shoulders squared.

"You failed." William's brown eyes blazed. "What makes you think we'd give you another chance?"

"You need the hybrid dead, don't you?"

Vlad moved as if to say something, but Méabh placed a hand on his arm and shook her head. She tilted her chin and observed the scene, but her expression gave no indication of her thoughts. Did she know of William's connection to the injured wolf? Darius couldn't be sure, but William's careful choice of words through the proceedings led him to believe not.

"We need discretion," William growled. "Something you've clearly demonstrated you're not capable of."

Shayan sneered. "Let's see how discreet I can be when I rip your throat out, wolf." His body started to turn translucent as shadows danced around him.

Diana stepped forward and whispered a word that was unintelligible to Darius's ears, removing the barrier that protected Shayan from his gold bonds. Immediately the Mist dropped to his knees, his body becoming solid as he arched back and screamed.

Within seconds, he seemed to wither and weaken. He slumped to the floor, his muscles taut from the agonising onslaught of the gold.

"Stop!" Maj yelled, stepping forward. "Give me the location. I'll finish this."

Darius watched the conflict rage on William's face. He was counting on the wolf to be the weak link. Would he allow another attack now that he knew about Ethan? The wolf stayed quiet, and beside him, something that looked suspiciously like satisfaction glinted in Méabh's eyes.

"All agreed?" Vlad looked at each of the Council members, then nodded to Maj. "Make sure it's done properly this time."

Diana whispered another unintelligible word and Shayan fell silent on the floor. She stepped back in line with the Council and pulled up the hood of her cloak.

23

Lily worried at the skin around her thumbnail as she paced the empty training room. Her hand subconsciously reached for her phone again. For the third time in as many minutes, she glanced at the blank screen. It had been forty-eight hours; surely it should be done by now. Why hadn't they contacted her?

She clutched her canvas bag to her midsection and fought the urge to scream until her throat was raw. She'd kept the Ouroboros close ever since she'd given Diana the location. Its familiar weight was a small comfort as she counted the minutes until her nightmare was over. One little phone call; that was all she needed.

"So, how did you get it?" Shade's voice came from behind, startling her out of her thoughts.

"What are you talking about?" Her brow furrowed in confusion as she tried to make sense of the question. How long had he been there? Had he been watching her?

He nodded to the bag she held. "The Ouroboros. I'm guessing it's the same one."

Her heart stopped. Icy blue eyes bore into her and she fought the sudden need to fidget.

"I don't know what you mean." Her voice was calm but her hand jerked involuntarily on the bag, clasping it tighter. She angled her body away from him in a vain attempt to block the bag from sight.

"Yes, you do. And I can even guess why you have it. But trust me, Lily, there's no good way to come back from the dead."

Anger flared white hot in her chest, overshadowing the fear and uncertainty. "You don't know what you're talking about."

His laugh held no trace of humour and his voice was bitter when he said, "Oh, don't I?"

She shook her head; she wasn't interested in his lecture. His opinion didn't matter now anyway.

"I don't know what you *think* you saw, but I don't have an Ouroboros. Do you really believe I'd be standing here wasting time with you if I could go back and make it all right?" Despite her best efforts, her voice cracked, and something akin to pity flashed across his face.

"I think you're a scared young girl who's gotten in way over her head. And if you're not careful, there'll be no way back."

Her hackles rose and defiance pulled her shoulders back and made her stand tall. "How about you stay out of my business, Shade."

She turned to stalk away, only to find Abi walking towards them, concern creasing her brow. Lily's breath caught as she scanned the girl's face for any sign of grief. Shade grew completely still beside her.

Abi's gaze flicked warily between them. "Is everything okay?"

Lily hesitated for a second before looking to Shade, only to find the vampire walking away without giving them another glance.

Abi placed a hand on her arm and frowned. "Lily, what did he say to you? You're shaking."

"He ... he was saying there's no good way to come back from the dead."

"What the hell does that mean? Was he threatening you?"

She shook her head, but then paused and glanced uncertainly at Abi. She could feel the anger and need to protect radiating off the other girl and a thought flirted at the back of her mind. What was one little lie in the grand scheme of things? One more little sin on her way to hell.

"He was talking about witches being untrustworthy. That we were too easily corrupted by dark magic or some crap like that. I just pointed out that if it hadn't been for the vampires ..." She shrugged and looked at the ground. "He got pretty mad when I mentioned Darius."

Out of the corner of her eye, she could see Abi frown. An uncomfortable knot twisted in her stomach, and she dug her nails into the palms of her hands to stop herself from backtracking. She hadn't said anything really, just a distraction; that's all.

"Shade was abandoned by his Sire when he was turned, wasn't he?" Abi chewed her lip thoughtfully. "Where was it you said he's from?"

She shrugged. "Dublin, I think."

"So, he was sired in Darius's territory."

Silence hung in the air between them and Lily dug her nails in harder.

Abi plastered a smile on her face. "I better check in with Phoenix; I haven't heard from her since last night."

24

———

Heavy black clouds rolled across the sky, and Phoenix's hands clenched involuntarily on the leather steering wheel at a sudden bang of thunder. She wasn't sure how long she'd been driving for, but at some stage between leaving the B&B and navigating the winding country roads, the bright morning sun had shifted to an ominous and oppressing sky that mirrored her mood.

Ethan had yet to move as he lay across the back seat of the car, and fear had her heart tightly in its clutches. If it wasn't for the fact he remained in wolf form, she'd have long ago succumbed to her fear and brought him to the nearest hospital. Since bringing him to a vet was also out of the question, she took what comfort she could from the steady beat of his heart and kept driving. He'd wake up. He had to.

The question now was where was she driving to? The logical thing would be to contact the others and get their help. But what if she led the danger right to them? The Mist had almost killed both her and Ethan. She couldn't ask anyone else to put themselves at risk.

She couldn't stick to their original plan either; if the Mist found them at the last B&B, it would be stupid to assume he wouldn't find them at the next. Which only left Ethan's pack.

They'd be in the best position to help with Ethan's injuries, and Cormac had already offered her his protection. But still she hesitated. The whole point of their little jaunt around Ireland was to limit how much trouble they were bringing to the pack's door. If she headed there now, she'd be bringing a whole lot more than trouble – she'd be bringing death.

So, she drove in the general direction of north, sticking to back roads and isolated locations, all the while urging Ethan to wake up so she didn't have to make the decision alone.

Another clash of thunder sounded overhead and moments later, thick droplets of rain pelted her windscreen. The pounding beat was so deafening, she almost missed the ringing of her phone on the passenger seat beside her.

She glanced at the screen and her breath caught when she saw "unknown number". Her old phone had been left back in Dublin as a temporary decoy for anyone who might be tracking it. Only a handful of people had this number, and all of their names should have come up on the screen.

The phone continued to vibrate insistently, and she swung the car into a gravelly lay-by that came up on her left. She fumbled to pick it up and pressed the answer button before the car had come to a complete stop. Heart pounding, she said nothing as she lifted the phone to her ear.

"I know you're there, Phoenix."

The familiar voice that came down the line sent a wave of nausea flooding through her and the world spun.

"How did you get this number?" The words came out in a whisper rather than the furious demand she'd intended.

Darius's rich laugh sent shivers down her spine and the nausea faded, only to be replaced by a confused mix of sadness and anger.

"I have my ways. Don't worry. I'm not looking to hurt you. I could've done that long before now if it had been my desire."

She sneered, his words adding fuel to her anger. "Of course not. You need me alive for the prophecy, after all."

"Exactly."

Her free hand clenched the steering wheel so tightly, the leather creaked in protest under her grip. Why was she even humouring this conversation? She already knew he was insane. But before she could force herself to hang up, Darius's tone shifted from chilling psychopath to the charming persuasion she'd always known him for.

"I'll admit I'm quite impressed you managed to survive Shayan's attack. That's no meagre feat. The Council, however, were less impressed and intend on sending the next Mist." He let the statement hang in the air for a moment. "I wish to offer you my protection."

She choked, his words causing a shocked laugh to bubble up in her throat. "Your protection?"

"You were lucky with Shayan. Maj is neither as naive or careless. And, should you by some miracle survive her,

Jannah will crush you like a bug. As you quite succinctly pointed out, it is in both of our interests that you survive. Therefore, I propose a temporary truce."

"You seriously think I would ever accept help from you?"

"I think you want to live. I'll give you some time to consider my offer, but I advise you do so quickly. I'll be in touch."

With that, he hung up and Phoenix was left staring numbly at a blank screen as her hands trembled.

Phoenix huddled over the cup of coffee, as if its warmth might somehow chase away the chill that had settled in her centre. The watery brown liquid tasted like scorched piss and did little more than burn her tongue, but still she clung to it.

The rain had grown even heavier, teeming in sheets of water that made visibility non-existent and turned the treacherous country roads into a death trap when combined with her frazzled nerves. So, when she'd come across the ramshackle building that passed itself off as a petrol station, she'd done the sensible thing and pulled in.

Her automatic response after the call from Darius had been to drive, as if by doing so she could put distance between herself and the memories conjured from the mere sound of his voice. Some things you just couldn't outrun, however, and now that she'd been forced to stop, she felt lost.

Was what he said true? Was the Council sending

another Mist? The first had been bad enough, and she couldn't deny it had been anything other than pure luck that kept them alive, but a second one just added yet more unknowns she wasn't ready to deal with alone.

She blew out a breath and rested her head on the steering wheel. Hell, when had she become so reliant on other people that her biggest fear out of that whole scenario was the part where she was alone?

As if in response to her thought, her phone vibrated on the passenger seat. Her stomach did a full three-sixty and threatened to return its contents for visual inspection as she flipped the phone over to see the screen. This time, a familiar name flashed persistently back at her and her head swam with relief.

"Abi," she answered breathlessly.

"Phoenix? Are you okay?" Abi's cheery voice took on a panicked edge, and Phoenix forced herself to take a slow, deep breath before answering.

"Yeah, sorry. I thought it was someone else calling. I ... It's just good to hear your voice."

"What's going on? And don't say nothing. I can tell you're upset."

Phoenix leaned back in the driver's seat and closed her eyes for a moment. "The Council found us. They sent one of their assassins. We barely managed to escape. And then Darius called. He said they're sending another one to finish the job. He wanted to offer me his protection; a temporary truce, he said. Is he completely insane? How could he ever think I'd trust him after everything he's done?"

The flood of words came to an abrupt halt, and she was

suddenly aware of the stunned silence on the other end of the phone.

"Shit," was Abi's only response.

Phoenix started laughing. And as her friend joined her, an invisible weight lifted from her chest. The laughter turned to a hysterical fit of giggles until tears were rolling down her cheeks and she was no longer sure if they were good tears.

"I'm afraid, Abi," she whispered when she was finally spent and the energy drained from her body.

"It's okay to be afraid, just as long as you don't stop fighting. Now, first things first, where are you?"

She looked around at her grey, nondescript surroundings and suddenly felt the heavy weight of exhaustion settle over her. "I'm not sure. Up north somewhere. I just kept driving."

"Okay, let's start by getting you guys somewhere safe. Can you find a B&B nearby? Text me your location. I'll fill the others in. Nate hasn't managed to get past the Council's firewalls yet, so we can't verify what Darius said, but maybe he can find out how Darius got your number."

Abi rattled off orders, asking questions about the assassins and the Council's attack. Phoenix could tell that the calm, assured tone was an act for her benefit but at that moment, she was immensely grateful for her friend's strength.

"There's something else," she said once she had answered all of Abi's questions. "Ethan –"

A flash of lightning lit the sky and the line went dead. She gaped at the "no signal" sign on the phone and cursed.

She was jinxed; she had to be. There was no other explanation for it.

A shuddering gasp from the back seat made her jump, and she spun around to see the final patches of fur fade from Ethan's now human body. His eyes fluttered open for a brief second, then closed, leaving her alone once more.

25

Lily methodically folded her clothes and placed everything into a neat pile, ready to go. Surely it wouldn't be long now. Diana would call to give her the green light, and she'd take the Ouroboros to the Council. They'd show her how to tap into its powers and she'd fix everything; it would be over.

The door to her room burst open, and she jerked her head up in surprise to see a frazzled Abi standing there.

"The Council found them." Abi had hardly finished blurting out the words before she turned on her heel and disappeared again.

Lily froze, staring at the space where the girl had been. *Was it was done?*

Heart racing, she lurched into action. She ran out into the hallway to find Abi pounding on Nate and Shade's doors. Lily ground to a halt as she took in the other girl's expression. There was no sign of grief, only a barely contained urgency.

How could there be no grief? If Phoenix was dead, there should be grief.

When there was no answer from either room, Abi swung back to her. "How could they have known?"

"What? Wait –" Lily held up her hands as much to pause her own racing thoughts as to calm the other girl down. "What are you talking about? How could who have known?"

"The Council!" Quickly, Abi relayed her phone call with Phoenix. "How could they have known?" she repeated. "We didn't tell anyone the plan. No one knew where they'd be."

Lily's pulse pounded so loud she was sure even Abi's human hearing would pick it up. Phoenix was alive. The Council failed.

"What about Darius?" she suggested numbly, her thoughts racing. "You said he contacted her. Maybe he's really working for the Council?"

Abi shook her head, but before she could say anything further, footsteps sounded at the far end of the hall.

Nate and Shade rounded the corner, deep in conversation. They pulled up short when they spotted the two girls standing in the corridor and took in the tension that was an almost palpable force in the air. Shade scowled, his frosty gaze fixing on Lily, while Nate hurried to their side.

"What's going on?" he demanded.

Lily's hands grew clammy as Abi recounted her conversation with Phoenix. She watched the cogs turning in Nate's head, sure that any minute now he'd realise what she'd done and turn to her with the same look of accusation that was clear as day in Shade's eyes.

"Okay, first things first. We need to assume the Council knows our plans," Nate said, jolting her out of her panicked thoughts. "Which means we need to change them. Let me make a few calls. You guys get your shit and be ready to leave as soon as I've got another safe house sorted."

"What about Ethan and Phoenix?" Shade demanded, finally shifting his gaze from her.

"Phoenix sent you their new location?" Nate looked to Abi for confirmation. "They should be safe for now, but I'm not so sure it's a good idea for them to be on their own anymore."

"They need more help," Shade agreed.

A strange look passed between Nate and Shade, and Lily's stomach lurched. Had Shade said something to Nate already? Was that why he wasn't coming straight out and voicing his accusations?

"We don't have much time. We need to move." With that, Nate hurried off to make arrangements. Shade gave her a final glare and followed after him.

Lily watched them go and tried to calm the panic that was bubbling up inside of her. "Excuse me," she muttered to Abi, mumbling a vague excuse about needing to do something before they left.

She made a beeline for the nearest exit and pushed through the door. The cold hit her with a sharp slap, and through her muddled thoughts, one fact came into sharp focus: it wasn't over. Needing answers, she pulled out her mobile and pressed the call button, only dimly aware of the ringtone as she wandered aimlessly around the property's grounds.

"Lily, I was going to call you later today," Diana answered, her voice warm and friendly.

"What's going on? Why isn't it done?" Lily could hear

the frantic edge in her tone, but she couldn't seem to calm the emotions that raged through her.

There was a long pause, then Diana sighed.

"I'm afraid there was a slight miscalculation in our tactics. But it's nothing for you to worry about. It's all in hand. All I need is the next location from you and I'll get it sorted. This horrible mess will all be over."

Lily hesitated. She wanted so much to feel reassured. The Council had it all under control; she just needed to let them handle it. So why didn't she feel relieved?

"I know how hard this is for you." Diana's voice softened. "But I need you to be strong a little while longer. Annabelle needs you to be strong. You can do that, can't you? For Annabelle?"

Her throat tightened at the sound of her sister's name. Where was Annabelle now? So much time had passed. Too much. Had her soul already passed on to a new life? Would she be too late?

Before she could think any further, she spurted out the address that Phoenix had sent Abi and hung up without saying goodbye. Hot tears pricked the back of her eyes, but she refused to let them fall. Tears wouldn't help her now.

26

Everything went white. Then there was only darkness, never-ending darkness. Ethan could hear Phoenix's voice, whispering to him, begging him to come back to her. But no matter how hard he tried to pull himself out of the murky swamp of his thoughts, reality remained just out of his reach. The harder he tried, the more fatigue washed over him and brought with it the emptiness of oblivion.

A light touch to his cheek sent a jolt of awareness through him. His skin tingled as fingertips trailed along his forehead and smoothed the tension from his brow. The warm scent of sunshine flooded his senses, and his eyes fluttered open to meet the most striking green eyes he'd ever seen. They tightened with worry until they registered his own brown ones staring back.

A small smile lifted the corner of Phoenix's mouth and she sat back, taking her hand and her warmth with her.

"Hey."

"Hey." His response came out as little more than a croak, and she jumped up to grab him some water.

The room tilted at an odd angle as he watched her, and it took a minute for the fuzziness to clear enough for him to realise he was lying down. The magnolia walls blended into the magnolia ceiling above his head, and the musty smell that filled his nose was unfamiliar. Where were they?

Phoenix came back into his line of sight with a glass of water in hand. He made a weak attempt to shift his body to a sitting position, but she glared a warning at him. Quickly and efficiently, she propped a pillow up behind him and moved him enough that she could hold the glass to his mouth for a few sips.

"You will not so much as blink until we know what damage has been done," she ordered as she fussed about to make sure his body was fully supported.

Her words triggered a flash of memory: a hand reaching into his chest, and pain, blinding pain. He winced.

"The Mist –" He swallowed with effort past the uncomfortable dryness in his throat. "I'm guessing you didn't win him over with your charms. How are we alive?"

She arched an eyebrow at him and the tension that had tightened her features was instantly replaced with a challenging smile. "Are you sure? I'll have you know that I can be very charming."

He choked on a laugh. "I'll believe it when I see it." The memory of the fist clenched around his heart flashed into his mind again and he grew sombre. "Tell me."

Her eyes darkened and she quickly averted her gaze from his, but not before he caught a glimpse of her haunted expression.

"I don't know. I just remember grabbing you and calling the sun. There was a burst of white light and next thing I know, I woke up in the woods to find you unconscious beside me. The Mist was gone."

"Dead?"

"What are the chances we'd be that lucky?"

He sighed. She was right, and going by what she said, it was little more than a miracle they were alive. In fact ... he took a mental inventory of his injuries: crippling fatigue unlike anything he'd felt before, phantom ache in his chest, raw throat. But no sign of burns. If she was holding him when she used her powers, he should have been incinerated. How was he alive?

"Where are we?" Too exhausted to think on it further, he focused on the practicalities.

Even if the Mist was by some miracle dead, there were two more at the Council's disposal; it was only a matter of time before they came.

Phoenix looked around, dazed, as if his question confused her.

"A B&B up north. I got a call and ... when you changed back, I thought it was best to get you some place comfortable."

He studied her closely. Why had she hesitated?

"Do the others know what happened?"

She shook her head. "The storm knocked out my phone signal when I was filling Abi in. The weather seems to have gone a little bat shit crazy all of a sudden. I texted her our location when the signal came back, and I was just about to give her a call."

For some strange reason, her answer relieved him. It wasn't that he wanted to lie to the others, but if people knew he was out of action, they'd also know Phoenix was more vulnerable. That was the last thing they needed right now. The fact he felt like a failure was irrelevant; it was her safety he was thinking about.

"Let's keep it to ourselves for the moment. No need to worry them unnecessarily."

She raised her eyebrows in surprise but didn't push further. Instead, she chewed her lip and started pacing. Her eyes flicked nervously to the drawn curtains that hid their room from anyone passing outside the window. Then a hesitant glance in his direction.

"Ethan ... Darius called."

***

Darius stepped through the portal and into his office in the Club of Night. He brushed his hands down his black suit and grimaced at the lingering magic that prickled across his senses. He was growing very tired of jumping every time the Council clicked their fingers. If it wasn't for the patience he'd cultivated through centuries of planning, he'd have long ago given up the charade of being a loyal puppy.

But perception was everything, and it was important that he control theirs. His Sire had learned the hard way what happened when control was lost; he wouldn't make the same mistake.

A sharp rap on the door signalled the arrival of his head of security. Raphael's replacement was a solid wall of muscle and composure. He didn't have quite the same psychotic tendencies as his predecessor, which ironically made him a better choice to oversee the security of their operations, if a less fun one.

"Erik, tell me you've found her."

The vampire gave a curt nod. "The wolf has been surprisingly efficient in tracking the hybrid and her canine companion. Are you certain the link to his pack is severed?"

Darius steepled his fingers and raised a neatly manicured eyebrow. Maybe it had been worth losing the insanity in his right-hand man for the benefit of clear, intelligent thinking.

"Our tests indicate as much, but keep a close eye on our dear Sean. The Omega's desire to protect the other wolves does not mean he's loyal to our cause."

Another sharp nod.

"What about the demon? Is everything set up for the experiment?"

"All ready to go. You just need to confirm which species you want to use as the host."

Anticipation pushed away some of his mounting frustration. Which to use? Some were more expendable, but others were more conducive to the final end game.

"Run the first trial on one of the vampires," he decided. "If they take well, we can proceed straight to the next stage."

The thought made him shiver with excitement and his fangs descended. He licked the edge of one and cast a quick glance at his Rolex. No time for a treat just yet. Maybe later, once he made sure Phoenix didn't get herself killed.

"Get me the co-ordinates for the hybrid and have some of our top men on standby. I may need some assistance if Maj arrives before I do."

"Done." Erik held the door to the office open for his boss and followed as he headed for the black Mercedes waiting in front of the club. "I take it she didn't accept your offer of sanctuary?"

Darius's smile was cold in response. "No, but she'll soon see the error of her ways. And if she doesn't, we can always use our leverage to convince her."

27

Phoenix eased the bathroom door closed as she slipped quietly back into the bedroom and tried not to disturb Ethan. He was so still on the bed that her gut clenched in a moment of panic before she could focus on the steady beat of his heart. She'd come so close to losing him.

It was a good sign that he'd regained consciousness, but she couldn't help worry about the ashen tone to his normally tanned skin, and the light sheen of sweat that coated his forehead. Even a brief conversation that afternoon had exhausted him, and he'd been resting since.

"You don't have to wait until I'm asleep to ogle me," he mumbled. His lip quirked up in a cheeky grin even as his eyes stayed closed.

She scowled at him and turned to the dressing table to plug in the small kettle. "I just wanted to make sure you hadn't wussed out on me and kicked the bucket."

"Aw, would you miss me?" He peeked one eye open and his grin widened, softening his deathly appearance somewhat.

"Yeah, about as much as I'd miss having my fingernails pulled out."

Ignoring the satisfied look on his face, she grabbed two tea bags and threw them into the paper cups provided by the B&B before filling both with water. Three sugars later and hers was just how she liked it. Ethan's she plopped unceremoniously on the bedside table beside him.

He looked up at her with pathetic puppy dog eyes. With a mock sigh, she turned back to the tea station to grab some of the individually wrapped biscuits. She flung two at him, then sat down in the armchair beside the bed, hugging her knees to her as she cradled the tea between her hands.

"Did you manage to reach Abi?"

"Hmm?" She looked at him in confusion for a minute. "Oh, yeah. I called her while you were asleep. They're getting ready to move to another safe house Nate has organised."

"You okay?" Ethan's forehead creased in concern as he watched her.

She gave him a wry smile. "Shouldn't I be asking you that?"

Without answering, he shifted over in the bed and shuffled his way up to a semi-reclined position. "Sit. Talk to me." He patted the empty space beside him.

She bristled at the order and opened her mouth to tell him to get stuffed, but was once again struck by just how fragile he looked. The simple process of clearing a space for her seemed to have worn him out completely as he leaned back against the headboard for support.

Softening, she scooched out of the chair and onto the bed beside him. The bed was large; two singles pushed together and covered with oversized sheets to make it appear as one – assuming you didn't roll into the dip in the middle. Even still, she was conscious of the heat of his body at her side.

They sat in silence for a few minutes, him getting his strength back from the small effort and her musing on just how fucked up her life had become while pointedly ignoring the way his musky scent made her head swim.

"It couldn't have been easy hearing his voice."

Her heart gave a pained spasm as she remembered Darius's call. She had no doubt left that he was evil, but it seemed her heart still hadn't quite come to terms with the revelation.

"You know the funny thing? He wanted to help me." Her laugh was bitter as she leaned against the headboard. "He said the Council was sending the next Mist and he needs me alive." Her throat burned. "He offered me sanctuary."

"No!" Ethan lunged forward, his eyes flashing yellow for a split second before he collapsed back.

Her jaw dropped in surprise at his almost feral response. "Well, of course I wasn't going to take him up on it." She gave him her best "well, duh" look as she helped him fix the pillow behind his body for support.

He blew out a slow breath with a sheepish grin. "Sorry, I didn't mean it like that. It's just the thought of him coming anywhere near you ..."

His eyes darkened as they examined her face. Uncomfortable with their intensity, she averted her gaze to focus on her fidgeting hands. He wrapped a hand around hers to still their nervous twitching. His one hand was large enough to cover both of hers and so much warmer than her own naturally cool temperature. The heat seeped from his skin into hers, and the chill that had started with the mention of Darius began to ease.

Her instinct was to pull away from the comfort he offered, but the weight of his hand was oddly reassuring. Instead, she leaned back against the headboard once more and rested her head next to his.

They sat like that for a while before he turned to her with a puzzled look on his face. "How did he get your number?"

She tensed and pulled her hands from beneath his. The question had been running through her mind ever since Darius called. Not to mention the still unanswered question of how the Council found them at the last B&B. Only a handful of people knew where they'd be, and those same people were the only ones with her number. The thought made her uneasy in a way she couldn't quite explain. And it didn't help that Abi had – hesitantly – raised some concerns when she spoke to her earlier that evening. But she had a strange feeling Ethan wasn't going to appreciate her thoughts on the subject.

"Only our group has this number. I made sure of it."

"Well, we know none of them would have given it to him."

She looked at him, searching for any kind of doubt on his face. There was nothing but certainty.

When she didn't immediately respond, he frowned. "Surely you don't think –"

A part of her wanted to just agree with him and shut her mouth. No matter how hard she tried, she couldn't think of a way to voice her concerns that wouldn't piss him off.

"Abi asked me something earlier that got me thinking." She bit her lip, trying to think past the little voice in her head that was begging her to just stay quiet. "If Shade was turned in Dublin, he'd be under the rule of the Dublin vampire clan, wouldn't he?"

Ethan shifted away from her ever so slightly, his expression hardening. "What are you saying?"

"I'm not saying anything. I'm just asking a question. He's never liked me. You can't deny that."

"That doesn't mean he'd ever help Darius."

"What about the Council?"

A heavy silence followed as she finally voiced the thought that had been niggling at the back of her mind. Ethan was right. It was unlikely Shade would help Darius if he truly had been the one to abandon him. But the Council was a different story. If he helped them, he not only got to ruin Darius's plans for world domination, but it also had the added bonus of getting rid of her. She could see him jumping for glee at that prospect – or at least cracking a smile.

"There's a big difference between disliking someone and wanting them dead. Shade has been nothing but loyal," Ethan eventually responded.

"To you, perhaps." She clenched her jaw and pushed off the bed. "I should've known there was no point trying to talk to you about this. I'm going out. I need some air."

She grabbed her jacket and flung open the door to the room.

"Phoenix –"

His protest was cut off with the slam of the door behind her.

Would it have really killed him to hear me out?

Phoenix shoved her hands into her jacket pocket and bent her head as the wind whipped around her with an angry howl. Trees bowed under the force and heavy, black clouds overhead promised more rain to come.

Hell, even Abi could see Shade had a bad attitude. Not Ethan, though. He just thinks Shade's the golden boy because he didn't turn into a blood fiend. Well, maybe that's because someone was keeping him in check all along. Maybe the sob story about his Sire is exactly that – nothing more than a story.

Aimlessly, she followed the dirt path that wound from the back of the B&B to a small lake, her only goal to put some distance between herself and Ethan. The biting wind was sharp against her face and the muddy waters swirled restlessly.

With a low rumble, the sky opened. Fat droplets pelted her from all angles and broke the flat surface of the lake. Within seconds, her hair was plastered to her face and she bore a stark resemblance to a washed-up rat.

Damn you, Ethan.

This was all his fault. If the stubborn fool had been capable of having a mature conversation, she wouldn't be standing out here freezing her wet arse off. Alone. When lethal assassins were trying to kill her –

Shit, what am I doing?

She sighed and shoved the hair out of her face. The

thought of going back really grated on her, but it would be pretty hard to make a point if she ended up dead. She'd just have to suck it up for now ... Or hide in the bathroom.

She was about to turn around when a warning prickle ran down her spine. She spun around, braced for an attack, and froze. A tall figure stood under a nearby tree, watching her. His profile was as familiar as her own, and she didn't have to see his face to recognise him.

Darius.

Her heart did that awful stutter again, and her breath stalled. He made no move towards her, but she found her feet glued to the spot as she stared at the man she'd considered family, and all thoughts of the torrential rain evaporated.

Of course, the water seemed to simply glide off his tailored suit while his black hair held perfectly in place, impervious to the blustery wind. The only thing in any way flawed about him was the subtle hint of scarring on the left side of his face. Scarring she'd caused.

"I thought it was time we spoke in person." His rich voice reached her despite the distance and the pounding of the rain.

"I've nothing to say to you."

Darius inclined his head and gave her a knowing smile. "I wouldn't be so sure of that. I came to warn you. The second Mist is on her way. I'd advise you leave quickly. She won't be as easily deterred as her brother."

Icy fear ran through her at the mention of the Mist, and she couldn't stop herself from giving a quick scan of her surroundings.

"I've already told you what you can do with your so-called protection." She crossed her arms defiantly, but inwardly winced at the slight tremor of her voice.

"Indeed. And I've no doubt you mean it. For now. But I'm confident that in time you'll come to me willingly. If I can find you this easily, what chance do you think you stand against the Council?"

His words cut straight to the quick, and she pulled her anger tightly to her as if it could act as a shield from the truth. "How did you find me?" she demanded.

"I have my sources. You really should be more careful who you associate with, you know."

Her breath caught in her throat and she became deathly still. The suspicion that had been plaguing her sent a chorus of butterflies fluttering around her stomach. Words turned to ash on her tongue as she battled with herself on whether or not to ask the next question. She already knew she couldn't trust a word he said, but she couldn't help herself; she needed to know.

"He's one of yours, isn't he? It was you that sired him."

Darius said nothing, just gave her a knowing smile. She felt an insatiable urge to put a fist through his smug face.

A loud rumble rolled through the sky, and a flash of lightning struck the ground mere feet from where she stood. She jumped back in surprise, adrenaline shooting through her as she prepared again for an attack. None came.

Just as suddenly as it had begun, the rain stopped, and when she looked towards Darius again, she found nothing other than an empty space where he'd stood.

Ethan leaned his head back against the headboard and closed his eyes. He growled, not even sure who he was more frustrated with, himself or Phoenix. No, Phoenix. It was definitely Phoenix.

She was so bloody stubborn. Trying to make her see sense was like talking to a brick wall. Only the brick wall didn't talk back.

Was it really so hard for her to see the good in people? Or at least see something other than the worst?

A bone-deep weariness filled him, and his whole body felt heavy. It had been almost twenty-four hours since the Mist's attack, and the slightest movement still left him panting for breath. His body should have healed by now.

The Mist. Shit! He bolted upright, sluggish brain cells finally making the connection that should have been blaring warning bells at him. Phoenix was out there alone and the next Mist was coming.

His heart hammered in his chest as he pushed the blanket off and swung his legs over the side of the bed. The room swam and the edges of his vision turned black. He closed his eyes and took slow, deep breaths until the world stopped tilting.

Luckily, he was already wearing jeans and a t-shirt because he didn't think he had the energy to get dressed. He just had to put shoes on; that should be easy enough.

As he bent to retrieve one of his shoes from under the bed, he toppled forward, only just managing to catch himself on the armchair. Not so easy after all.

A couple of minutes, and a lot of cursing later, he had shoes on his feet and had somehow managed to stumble outside. Heavy black clouds hung overhead and rain soaked him through in seconds. The chill permeated his very core, but he used the cold to focus his foggy thoughts.

One step at a time, he moved sluggishly forward. The wind felt like a wall of resistance against him, and by the time he reached the dirt track, he was forced to stop. He panted as he leaned against a tree for support. Leaves rustled above his head and a large crow landed on the ground in front of him. Strange red eyes watched him with an eerie intelligence that made him freeze. He'd seen those eyes before.

The air around the crow shimmered, and Ethan blinked against the rain that blurred his vision. Between one blink and the next, the crow disappeared. In its place stood a black wolf with the same red eyes.

His own wolf stood to attention, and when the black wolf turned and trotted down the path towards the nearby lake, he gritted his teeth and stumbled along after it. More than once, his vision turned black, but his instincts screamed at him to push on. One foot in front of the other: left, right, left, right.

Exhaustion was like a leaden blanket draped over him, and each blink he took seemed to last longer than the previous. He was dimly aware of Phoenix's voice in the distance, but he couldn't make out what she was saying. Who was she talking to?

He tried to call out, but his words were swallowed by a crash of thunder. And then the world went black.

Phoenix held her breath as her eyes scanned the clearing around her. Darius would reappear any second. Or, if not him, the Mist. She was sure of it.

A minute passed. Then two. Nothing.

The longer she waited for the hammer to fall, the more tense she became. Had she really seen him at all? Maybe her overactive imagination was playing tricks on her, or she'd just finally lost her marbles.

Another loud rumble overhead sent the rain pelting down once more. Thick raindrops mingled with hardened lumps of hail. It took only a few knocks to the head before she came to her senses; why the hell was she standing there waiting for someone to kill her when she should be getting a head start?

She pushed the sopping strands of hair out of her face and moved tentatively in the direction of the B&B. The pounding rain made it hard to hear anything other than the symphony of nature, but she strained for the slightest noise and watched for any sign of movement. Her heart pounded in her ears with each step and she fought the urge to break into a panicked run.

Just as she rounded the corner and the B&B came into view, she noticed a dark shape half-obscured by the hedges and long grass that bordered the trail. What looked like a shoe peeked out of the overgrowth, and she edged forward for a better look.

It took her a second to recognise the shoe as Ethan's, and a second more to make out his unmoving form attached to it. Her stomach flip-flopped and she closed the gap between them in an instant. A multitude of terrifying scenarios ran through her head as she crouched down beside him. Had Darius hurt him? The Mist? What the hell was he even doing out of bed?

Her hands trembled as she shook him. "Ethan. Ethan, wake up, dammit."

The plea was met with a weak murmur, but his eyes didn't open. Despite the chill of the rain, his skin was feverish beneath her touch. Instead of the strong, sure rhythm she expected, his heartbeat was rapid but thready. She needed to get him out of here, and she needed to get him help.

With a grunt, she hoisted the dead weight of his upper body off the ground and manoeuvred him until he was half draped over her shoulder. The weight was significant as she put one foot under herself and pushed to standing. But it was more his size that posed the biggest hindrance. Talk about déjà vu.

"I thought it was meant to be the man carrying the damsel in distress," she groused as she trudged back up the dirt trail and hoped like hell no one saw them.

She didn't even bother heading for the room. Instead, she made a beeline straight for their car, where she once again slung Ethan's unconscious form across the backseat. Darius knew where they were now. There was nothing in that room worth facing him for. Plus, if he was to be believed, every second they stayed increased their odds of coming face to face with the next Mist. And that wasn't a scenario she was up to dealing with right now.

It wasn't until she'd gotten them on the road and a comfortable distance from the B&B that she allowed herself to take a breath. She glanced in the rear-view mirror at Ethan's still form, and her chest tightened with worry. A sheen of sweat coated his grey-tinged skin and his breathing was shallow. He shouldn't be like this; he should have healed long before now.

With a slight twinge of guilt for betraying her promise to Ethan, she pulled out her phone and called Abi on loud-speaker. As soon as her friend answered, she blurted out the rest of the information about the Mist attack – the part that had left Ethan gravely injured.

"I don't know what the Mist did or how he did it, but Ethan's body isn't recovering the way it should. I was hoping he'd get better but he's not, and I don't know what to do. If the next Mist comes, we're in serious shit."

Abi was silent at the other end of the phone, and Phoenix blew out a long, shaky breath.

"Okay," Abi said finally, "I'll speak to the others and see what we can find out about the Mists. It sounds like they've got some weird mojo at their disposal, so we'll need to figure out how to counteract it. And I do mean *we*, Phoenix. You're not doing this on your own any longer."

She opened her mouth to protest, but shut it just as quickly. She didn't want to do this on her own. She was tired of trying to figure shit out by herself. Her nerves were fried. Besides, she had a vampire to confront, and what better way to do that than to show him just how much damage he'd caused.

So, she agreed a fresh plan with Abi and hung up, feeling a mixture of relief and trepidation as she pulled onto the motorway with a clear destination.

"Where are we going?"

She jumped in surprise at Ethan's mumbled question. When did he wake up?

"The others are leaving for a new safe house shortly. We're going to take a detour and meet them there in the morning." She threw a quick glance in his direction before fixing her eyes on the road.

"Do they know I've been hurt?"

She nodded, not really sure whether he was looking or not. A weary sigh and some shuffling were the only response from the back seat. When she glanced in the rear-view mirror again, Ethan's eyes were closed and he sat with his head leaning against the window.

Her grip loosened on the steering wheel a touch when she sensed no anger from him, but her relief was immediately replaced by a twist of anxiety. She might have just avoided an argument with Ethan, but there'd be a lot more to come if she was going to confront Shade face to face about his betrayal.

29

Lily trudged into the kitchen, idly wondering if it was possible to die from exhaustion as she made herself yet another cup of bitter coffee. The walls of the safe house were starting to close in on her and if they didn't get moving soon, she was afraid she'd start screaming and not be able to stop. Then again, what did it matter where she was? The location was all the same to her. Once she got the confirmation that Phoenix was dead, she'd be heading straight to the Council to fix everything.

The waiting had her nerves frayed. Every time someone's phone rang, her stomach dropped and a wave of nausea rolled through her as she stole herself for the news that was sure to come. It was like being on a never-ending rollercoaster, blindfolded. She was trying to keep the end goal in sight, but it was getting harder and harder the more time passed.

The steaming cup was halfway to her lips when the sound of a phone ringing reached her ears from the living room next door. She froze, recognising Abi's now painfully familiar ringtone. Her heart jack-hammered in her chest as she waited for the cry of grief, or some sign that the deed was done. None came.

With a shuddering breath, she forced her feet to move one step in front of the other, out of the kitchen and into the hall. She paused at the open doorway of the living room where Abi stood completely still with her phone held to her ear. Unable to hear the other side of the conversation, Lily tried to read between the lines of the girl's furrowed brow and intense concentration.

After listening for a moment, Abi straightened up and strode purposefully from the room without even a glance in her direction. Before Lily could move to follow, Shade appeared in front of her, his face an unreadable mask.

"If he doesn't recover from this, it'll be your fault." He didn't wait for a response, just followed in Abi's wake, calling over his shoulder. "You're going to want to hear this."

An insidious thread of fear wove its way through her confused thoughts as she stared at his receding back. What had his vampire hearing picked up that she'd missed?

With clammy hands and a very bad feeling, she ran down the hall, stopping only when she caught up to them at the office Nate had commandeered for the duration of their stay.

A metal desk sat in the centre of the room, covered in an assortment of screens and gadgets that obscured Nate from view. Only the rapid tapping of fingers on the keyboard gave away his presence. Abi stood over his right shoulder with her arms crossed and lips set in a determined line as she stared at the screen.

Shade waited inside the door and pointedly ignored her as she stepped into the room. Lily returned the favour and moved closer to the computer for a better look. "What's going on?"

Nate shifted in his chair but didn't look up from the screen. "Ethan's been hurt."

"What?" The question came out in a whisper as the bad feeling turned into a churning pit in her stomach.

"He told Phoenix to keep it quiet so we wouldn't worry, but he was hurt when the first Mist attacked. He's not healing the way he should be."

A low, buzzing noise filled Lily's ears as she tried to make sense of the words. She slumped against the wall, her legs going weak beneath her.

"But he'll be okay, won't he?"

Abi gave her a sympathetic look that did little to soften the grim expression on her face. "Nate's trying to get as much information as he can so we know what we're dealing with. We're thinking the Mist left some kind of poison in his system. Maybe you can start researching spells that might help?"

Lily nodded absently, the buzzing in her ears growing louder. Abi was still talking, outlining the plan she'd agreed with Phoenix, but the words seemed distant.

Diana promised. She promised me no one else would get hurt.

While the others crowded around the computer and brainstormed ideas for dealing with the Mists, she slipped from the room with her phone gripped tightly in her hand. She barely made it out of earshot before she had pressed the call button.

Diana answered on the third ring. The warm greeting that, until now, had helped to calm and reassure Lily, this time left her numb.

"You said it'd just be her. That no one else would get hurt."

The line was silent for a moment.

"There are always casualties in war, Lily." Diana's voice turned cold and a deep chill settled in Lily's chest.

"We're not at war."

"Aren't we?"

"Ethan is innocent," she insisted. "He's trying to stop this thing, just like you. He's not healing, Diana. He's really hurt."

"The wolf got in the way. If he hadn't, this would be over now. You'd have your sister back and my witches would be safe."

The buzzing in her head turned to a barely contained scream as all the conflicting emotions fought for attention. Of course she wanted her sister back, dammit, but this wasn't right. Every part of her being was telling her this was wrong.

"I can't do this," she said quietly. Her final thread of hope faded and took a piece of her soul with it.

"I'm afraid it's too late for second thoughts now." Diana's voice turned hard, no hint of her earlier warmth and compassion remaining. "What will your friends think when they find out you betrayed them? Do you think they'd still accept you? You'd be even more alone than you are now. No, you *will* go through with this, Lily. And when it's over, you'll be reunited with your sister. Just like you wanted."

30

The morning sun was splitting the sky as Phoenix navigated the winding coastal road, finally en route to their destination after a long night laying diversions. The clear blue sky formed a surreal juxtaposition to the erratic thunderstorms of recent days and she raised her face, relishing the warmth of the sun as it beamed through the car's windscreen.

In the bright light of day, it seemed almost idyllic. Yet there was an energy to the place that she couldn't quite explain. She'd felt it as soon as they'd reached Portrush, and it had only grown stronger as they drew near their meeting point. It made all of her senses tingle, like a feather whispering across her skin. There was something both foreign and strangely familiar that called to her and pulled her in.

She debated asking Ethan if he felt the same thing, but an awkward silence had settled between them once he'd regained consciousness. There were so many things unsaid from their disagreement the night before, and they'd only increased in significance after her run-in with Darius.

She'd held off telling him about that little visit as well, needing to get her thoughts straight first. Soon she'd confront Shade herself and Ethan would have no choice but to believe her. The very thought made her gut twist painfully.

Beside her, now slumped in the passenger seat, Ethan gave a low whistle. She looked over at him, and her jaw dropped as they crested the hill and she was awarded a clear view of the ancient ruins that had caught his attention.

Dunluce Castle stood proud and imposing on the edge of the cliff. The sea was calm behind it, but an image filled her mind: waves crashing against the rocks as lightning split the sky. A shiver of anticipation ran through her.

Craning her head for a better look, she slowed the car as they neared the entrance. Coaches were parked along the grass verge and tourists milled about with cameras. They all seemed suitably impressed with the historic site, pointing and posing at random locations around the grounds. Were any of them aware of the immense power vibrating from the place? It was almost impossible to think that even the most mundane of humans could be oblivious to it.

"You feel it?" Ethan asked, his eyes glued to the castle as he sat up a little straighter.

She nodded even though he wasn't looking at her; she was too in awe to speak.

A car horn blared, snapping her from her trance. At some point, without realising, she'd slowed the car to a complete stop, and they were now blocking the narrow road with an irate driver making angry gestures behind them.

Ethan glanced at the car and gave her a somewhat dazed smile. "We better go meet the others. We can come back and explore later."

The rest of the drive was a blur. Colourful seafront houses came into view ahead and minutes later, the sat nav instructed them to turn into the drive of one of them. The mint green facade was a questionable choice of colour and the white paint surrounding the windows was cracked and flaking, but the views were stunning. Situated right on the seafront, she could easily imagine herself nestled behind one of the large bay windows, curled up with a cup of tea while watching the waves beat tirelessly against the rocks. It wasn't quite what she'd expected from the safe house.

Before she had two feet out of the car, the front door swung open and Abi sprinted down the driveway towards her. She braced herself to avoid being knocked over by her friend's enthusiastic embrace and laughed, hugging Abi back just as tightly. For a brief moment, her heart felt lighter than it had in days.

Nate and Lily followed Abi from the house, their expressions tight with concern. Her happiness soured a little as she saw them and realised Shade was no doubt waiting inside to avoid the morning sun. Her stomach twisted at the thought of the confrontation to come. Would the others take his side too?

Lily hurried to Ethan's door and helped him from the car. He tried to brush her off, but his movements were slow and laboured, even the smallest exertion causing a sheen of sweat across his forehead.

Abi cast a worried glance in his direction before turning back to Phoenix with a reassuring smile plastered on her face. "Come on. Let's get you inside."

Together they followed the others into the house and upstairs to the living room, which was ideally situated to make the most of the stunning views. Nate and Lily helped Ethan to the sofa, and Lily muttered something about a serum before scurrying out of the room.

Phoenix couldn't help but notice the lines of worry that now seemed permanently etched on the young girl's face as she passed by. Lily had lost weight in the short time the group had been apart, and her once tanned skin was almost as pale and sickly looking as Ethan's. The signs of grief were all too familiar to her now. She wished there was something she could say to take Lily's pain away, but no words could ease the loss; she knew that better than anyone.

"Did you manage to find anything that will help him?" Phoenix turned her concern to Ethan and frowned as she noticed the fist he held clenched over his sternum. He had his eyes closed, and the rise and fall of his chest was shallow as he fought to catch his breath.

"We think there might be some kind of poison in his system that's stopping him from healing." Nate's amber eyes met hers, worry depriving them of their usual sparkle. "Lily has put together a serum we hope will work, but we'll need you to melt some gold for us."

"Gold?"

"Yeah, we've found some references that indicate the

Mists react badly to it. We're hoping their magic will be the same." He shrugged. "Worst case scenario, it does nothing, but it won't hurt him to try. Not any more than he already is."

"*He* is still here, you know," Ethan grumbled but didn't open his eyes.

Phoenix bit her lip and looked around for Lily. How long did it take to prepare? She pushed back the niggling fear of what would happen if the serum failed. It would work; it had to.

Abi grabbed her hand and pulled her down to sit on the second sofa. Plump cushions swallowed her as if the sofa itself was trying to force her to relax. She didn't want to. She couldn't.

A large clock hung on the wall over an open fireplace, and she watched the second hand move around at a snail's pace. She was vaguely aware that Abi was telling her all about the training she'd been doing with Nate. She nodded in the appropriate places and gave her friend a weak smile, but her eyes were glued to Ethan. His whole body seemed tense, and she didn't miss his occasional winces of pain.

She'd just about had enough of waiting when Lily walked back into the room holding a glass full of greenish-blue liquid in one hand and a gold ring in the other. The girl's eyes flicked to Ethan and she flinched before looking to Phoenix.

"You ready?"

Lily closed her bedroom door with a soft click and rested her forehead against the cool wood. She scrunched her eyes tight and tried to force air into her lungs. Each breath she took pulled the invisible band tighter around her chest, and her head swam as she struggled for much-needed oxygen.

It was too much. Seeing Ethan's body spasm with the crippling pain that overtook him as the serum fought the poison in his system. It was all just too much.

She had no idea if the serum would work, and she'd been too much of a coward to stay and face the consequences of her actions. If he died, it would be her fault; she as good as murdered him herself. The knowledge twisted like a knife in her gut.

Silent tears streaked her cheeks and she slid to the floor, curling into a ball and hugging her knees to her. The pain in her chest increased, and she idly wondered if she was too young to have a heart attack. A dark place in the back of her mind welcomed the idea with relief.

The walls felt like they were closing in around her, and Diana's word echoed in her head. "It's too late for second thoughts now." This couldn't be the way she got her sister back. Annabelle would never want to be saved at the expense of someone else, least of all Ethan. And even if the Ouroboros managed to reset everything, could she live with herself, knowing the pain she'd caused?

She felt dirty, as if her insides were turning black with every lie and betrayal. She was losing a little bit more of herself each time; it felt like she was disappearing. A scream burned her throat as it tried to force itself free. She bit it back and clenched her fists in a vain attempt to hold it all in. She needed to fix this. She needed to make it right.

With a laboured breath, she pushed up from the floor and stumbled to the bed. She reached under the mattress for the white box before turning to the locker where her grimoire rested. The book lay open at the page she'd used for Ethan's serum, and the image of him contorted in pain once again flashed before her. She gritted her teeth and flicked past the page. That spell had already done its job; it would either work or it wouldn't. What she needed now was another spell, one that would help her end this.

Scrawled writing and roughly drawn images blurred past until she finally paused her search. Her breathing slowly returned to normal as she scanned the details. This was it. This was what she needed.

A strange sense of calm settled in her chest as she sat back on the bed and pulled the box onto her lap. She opened it and took a long look at the object she once thought would solve everything, then closed the lid and reached for her phone.

"I have your location," she said as soon as the call was answered.

31

Phoenix paced the length of the small kitchen as she waited for the kettle to boil. Adrenaline still flowed through her veins, setting her nerves on edge.

Ethan's response to the serum had been instantaneous and terrifying. Spasms had overtaken his whole body, and her heart had frozen in pure terror as she watched the veins bulge in his arms and neck, his back bowing. Her body had screamed at her to do something, but that was the problem, wasn't it? There wasn't always an enemy to fight. So, she'd watched helplessly as Nate held him down to stop him from hurting himself even more.

It had passed in a couple of minutes, but those minutes had been some of the longest of her life. What followed was a puke session worthy of a horror movie, but after that, Ethan's deathly pallor seemed to fade somewhat and his breathing had become less laboured. He fell into a deep sleep, which Nate assured her was a good thing. She still wasn't convinced.

Just as she was about to throw her cup at the wall, Abi popped her head through the door.

"He's awake."

Phoenix hurried after her friend and into the living room to find Ethan sitting up on the sofa, looking healthier than he had in days. He gave her a crooked smile and her heart stuttered in overwhelming relief.

"How are you feeling?"

"Better. Still pretty tired, but my body seems to be doing its thing now that whatever stopped it from healing is gone."

She slumped onto the sofa beside him, all the energy draining from her body along with the unspoken fear she'd clung to. She closed her eyes and allowed herself that moment to just breathe.

"We'll stay here until you get your strength back. Then we can all head to Donegal together," Nate was saying in the background.

Her eyes flew open as she suddenly remembered the other reason she'd been so determined for them all to regroup. "Where's Shade?"

She hadn't seen the vampire once since she'd gotten here. Her first priority had been to get Ethan help, but now that he seemed to be doing better, she didn't want to waste time playing happy families while Shade found another knife to stick in her back.

"He's gone to follow up on a possible lead that might help us with the Council," Nate answered.

On the sofa across the room, Abi shifted uncomfortably, not meeting her gaze. Ethan gave her a weary look and his brown eyes pleaded with her not to start an argument. She glared at him. How could he still believe that Shade was innocent?

Darius rats him out and suddenly he disappears to "follow up on a lead"? Come on, what a load of bullshit.

"Help us with the Council? Shade's working against us. He betrayed us to the Council, and he's the reason he" – she stabbed a finger emphatically in Ethan's direction – "almost got killed."

"Enough, Phoenix." Ethan sat forward, hanging his head in his hands as he propped his elbows on his knees. "You need to drop this ridiculous notion. Shade may not like you, but none of this is his fault."

"Darius confirmed it."

Ethan's head jerked up. "What?"

"Oh yeah, Darius paid me a little visit. Back at the B&B while you were having your catnap. He was only too happy to claim Shade as one of his own."

"What exactly did Darius say?" Nate asked, his tone far too reasonable for her liking despite the slight frown on his face.

She cast her thoughts back, trying to remember Darius's words. It was all a bit of a blur. Her emotions had been on such a rollercoaster since seeing him and the exhaustion was starting to cloud her mind.

"Does it matter how he phrased it? He confirmed that Shade was betraying us."

She waited for the lightbulb to switch on and understanding to dawn on their faces. But it didn't happen. Ethan just looked unbelievably weary, and even the slight downturn of Nate's mouth had relaxed. Only Abi appeared concerned by her words.

Nate gave her an apologetic shrug. "Sorry, Phoenix, but I don't buy it. Shade's a pain in the hole, but he's a good guy. We all know what Darius's word is worth."

She gaped at him, anger bubbling up inside her. "Are you shitting me? The guy was turned in Darius's territory and has some crock story about not knowing who his Sire is. And now he's disappeared just as Darius rats him out. How can you not see the connection here?"

Ethan sighed heavily. "It's not that we don't see your point, but you can't deny that your source is dubious at best. Even if Darius is his Sire, Shade is our friend. You can't really expect us to condemn him without even hearing his side of things."

A strange numbness filled her chest as she looked at each of them in turn. They didn't believe her.

With a stiff nod, she stood up. "I thought you might respect me enough to trust my word, but I guess I was wrong. If you want proof, I'll get it. I just hope no one else gets hurt while you hold on to your denial."

She turned and walked out of the room, nails digging into the palms of her hand as she swallowed past the burning in her throat.

Darius stepped through the portal and followed the rest of the Witnesses to the Council chambers. His face was a mask of indifference, but inside he was seething. A last-minute summons by the Council was an irritating show of power at the best of times, but this one had come at the most inconvenient moment.

Everything had been set up for the first test to transfer the demon. If the test was a success, not only would his plans take a significant leap forward, but he would also have a very useful weapon to help protect Phoenix from the Mists.

Low murmurs and restless shifting filled the antechamber. He caught snippets of conversation suggesting Maj had fulfilled her oath, and that was the reason for the sudden meeting. If not for the team he now had tracking Phoenix's movements, he'd have feared the same thing.

He hadn't exaggerated when he'd warned her the second Mist was coming. Less than an hour after she'd vacated the B&B, Maj had arrived. He'd watched from the shadows since there was no need for him to reveal himself just yet. Not surprisingly, there was no sign of Maj when he looked around the chamber. The Mist was a lot smarter than her younger brother and he strongly suspected she'd gone to ground to await her next opportunity rather than returning to admit failure.

And it was only a matter of time before that opportunity came. If Phoenix didn't come to her senses soon, it would make his job of keeping her alive a whole lot harder.

A sudden hush fell over the room, drawing his attention to the platform at the centre. All five Council members stood in a line with their hoods pulled low enough that their faces were cloaked in shadow.

The large double doors at the back of the room opened and Vicktor entered, making his way to the centre to stand before them. His pristine grey suit was complemented by his usual pompous air and arrogant confidence, but there was a subtle tension that held his shoulders a little too still.

To what do we owe the honour of this weasel gracing our presence yet again?

As Darius watched, Vicktor bowed his head and kept his gaze fixed to the ground until all Council members had lowered the hoods of their cloaks.

Méabh stepped forward with only a brief glance of acknowledgement for the CLO rep. "I'm sure you're all wondering why you've been summoned here at such short notice. It has come to my attention that one of our own has withheld key information from us. Information that may have contributed to a swifter end to this unfortunate situation."

Darius tensed, his eyes flicking back to Vicktor. Had the little weasel informed the Council of his involvement? He'd been sure the man would value his survival far too much to betray him. Not to mention it would risk bringing to light his own duplicitous actions. Had he been mistaken in not dealing with the rep sooner?

Vlad held up his hand to halt the intrigued murmurings filling the room. His face remained stoic, but there was a curious glint in his eye as he nodded for Méabh to continue.

She gave him a saccharine smile before turning to address the room once more. "The hybrid poses a threat to us all. And as such, it has been agreed that she must be sacrificed for the sake of the Lore and all humanity. We know from Shayan's failed attempt" – she cast a cold glance towards the youngest Mist who stood in the shadows scowling – "that there are others of our kind assisting her. With the help of key sources, we have managed to identify these accomplices."

She paused dramatically before nodding to Vicktor.

Vicktor straightened and smoothed invisible creases from his tailored suit jacket. "We at the CLO have been working tirelessly to gather information that may be of assistance to the Council in bringing this unfortunate matter to a swift conclusion. From our investigations, we can now confirm that, aside from the werewolf and witch, there is also a shifter and vampire aiding the hybrid in her endeavours. The concerning point, however, relates to the wolf. It appears that the man who intervened in Shayan's attack has a familial connection to one of the Council members."

He didn't have to speak the name for every eye in the room to turn to William.

The apologetic glance the CLO rep cast in the head werewolf's direction was as genuine as Darius's supplication to Council rule. William, for his part, didn't react. He held his hands clasped loosely in front of his body with his steely gaze fixed dead ahead.

Of course, this wasn't new information to him. Darius himself had seen to that. But it was obvious from the tension radiating from the other Council members that they'd been kept in the dark about this little fact.

Diana's eyes blazed as she crossed her arms. Vlad's expression didn't change so much as his energy shifted with a subtle movement of his body and a darkening in the colour of his eyes. Darius could clearly see the cogs turning in the vampire's mind.

Kam tilted his head and regarded his fellow Council member closely. It was he that stepped forward and called a hush to the rumble of speculation moving around the antechamber.

"William, would you care to speak in your defence?"

The wolf looked at him and a muscle jumped at the side of his jaw. Just once.

"What exactly am I expected to defend? I was as unaware of this connection as you. It changes nothing."

Diana gaped at him before snapping her mask of composure back into place. "Of course it changes things. How do we know you haven't been feeding him information?"

"I haven't."

She opened her mouth in retort, but William turned to address the other members of the Council before she could utter another word.

"As we've just heard, there is also a shifter" – he nodded towards Kam – "a vampire" – nod in Vlad's direction – "and a witch" – a pointed look at Diana – "helping the hybrid. My priority is as it's always been: the safety of our people. If a member of my family chooses to get themselves caught in the crossfire, that's their choice."

Darius raised an eyebrow as he watched the interchange. He knew the wolf was bluffing, and any other Supe in the room with a good nose should have also been able to smell the lie. Yet, William appeared completely assured, and the lack of condemnation from the crowd would suggest the Witnesses were sold on his declaration. *Interesting.*

"May I make a proposal?" Vlad held his arms wide and pasted the perfect politician smile on his face as he addressed the room. "The second Mist has already been deployed. It's only a matter of time before we receive confirmation that she has fulfilled her duty. Perhaps William might agree to remain within Council chambers until such a time we receive that confirmation ... Just a formality, of course. To put everyone's minds at ease regarding his loyalty."

William bared his teeth at the vampire, and Vlad's smile widened.

"That seems a fair proposal to me," Méabh agreed, a long red fingernail playing at the corner of her full red lips as she regarded William with a calculating gaze.

The other Council members nodded their agreement. William inclined his head in acknowledgement and stalked from the room.

33

Phoenix drove aimlessly, no real destination or plan of action in mind. It wasn't like you could outrun your own thoughts, was it? The numbness that had started in her chest now wrapped around her like a protective bubble and she clung to it, grateful for the temporary reprieve it afforded. She'd switched off her phone, too, but only after sending Abi a message to reassure her she was okay and promising not to leave without her.

Did she intend on leaving? She had no idea. Where would she even go? She just knew that somewhere under the protective layer of numb, she was angry. And hurt. Even with everything pointing to his guilt, they were taking Shade's side over hers. She was still the outsider, and he was their friend.

If she stayed and they stuck to the original plan, there was a high chance it'd put her in more danger. But when she thought of walking away, her stomach churned uncomfortably. Had she gotten so used to having others to rely on that she was afraid to be alone? Or was it the thought of walking away from Ethan?

As the sun dipped low on the horizon, she found herself drawn back to a familiar view: the castle.

At the edge of the jagged cliff, the setting sun framed the ruins in a glowing halo of red that seemed to pulse with the energy filling the air. She slowed the car to a crawl as she neared the entrance and watched the last coach of tourists pull away.

An old man in a green duffel coat and tweed cap pulled the barrier to the carpark closed, his movements painstakingly slow as he fitted the large padlock. When the lock clicked into place, he turned to look at her car, which was now stopped at the end of the dirt road, and inclined his head. Phoenix couldn't be sure from where she sat, but she could've sworn there was a satisfied look on the old man's face.

A glint in the distance drew her attention towards the cliff edge and she squinted, trying to see what had caused it. Nothing obvious jumped out at her, so she turned her gaze back to the gate to find the old man gone and the locked gate now open and waiting.

Curious, she put the car into gear and eased the car up the narrow dirt road. She killed the engine and got out, expecting to feel the bite of the salty sea breeze on her skin, but there was nothing. The air was unnaturally calm, and it held a weight that seemed almost pensive.

A strange vibration ran down her spine and thrummed through her solar plexus. She looked around, searching for a possible source, but she was completely alone.

Slowly, she walked towards the low stone wall that

formed a barrier between the carpark and lush green lawns of the castle. As she passed the rear of the car, the vibration turned into an odd tugging sensation, almost like an invisible rope was attached to her sternum, pulling her backwards.

She eyed the boot of the car warily and stretched an intrepid hand out to open it. She held her breath, half expecting something to jump out and attack, but the boot opened with an anticlimactic click.

A tentative peek inside revealed nothing other than the few belongings she and Ethan had brought with them: two rucksacks of clothes, some emergency supplies, and the wooden box covered in Celtic symbols that held her father's sword.

Her hand reached towards the box and the insistent pull grew stronger. She bit back a nervous laugh as she envisaged opening it to see the sword inside glowing. Thankfully, it wasn't.

When she lifted the lid, the sword sat innocently cushioned on the bed of red satin. The blade was as simple as the box was ornate. It was only with a closer look that similar Celtic designs could be seen shimmering along the metal. She wasn't fooled by its beauty, however – she knew the edge of that blade was razor sharp and utterly lethal.

Without a thought, her hand closed around the smooth wooden grip, and instantly a sense of calm fell over her. A tension she hadn't even fully acknowledged unravelled itself, and she took a deep breath. The salty air tickled her nose as she filled her lungs.

The bronze hilt sat snuggly against her hand, the long blade perfectly balanced. Shafts of light radiated from the sword when the sun's rays touched it, and for a moment, she was mesmerised. An answering heat came to life in the centre of her chest.

She took a step back in surprise at the visceral reaction of her body. Suddenly uneasy, she moved to place the sword back in its casing, but the vibration started again, more insistent this time. A heavy sense of foreboding replaced the heat in her chest and she swallowed, stepping away from the car with the sword still gripped in her hand.

All of her senses were on high alert as she stepped over the low wall. The grass beneath her feet was unnaturally green and luscious. Flowers dotted the fields around the castle in a spectrum of colours she'd never seen before, or at least not since she was a child following her mother around the garden. Power ran across her skin like static electricity and increased as she moved forward with careful steps.

What is this place?

As she reached the large stones that formed the boundary wall of the ruins, a gust of wind ruffled her hair. It carried the echoes of a soft lament, and she looked around in confusion for the source.

An unseen force urged her forward into the castle, and from one blink to the next, she found herself surrounded on all sides by thick stone walls – or what remained of them anyway.

The sword vibrated in her hand once more and she raised it, testing the weight. Though she'd never held this particular sword before, it felt like the most natural thing in the world to let the blade move through the pattern of movements her father had taught her many years before.

The air shimmered, and she stared, hypnotised by the iridescent trail it left.

She was so entranced by the sight that everything else around her faded until a familiar voice called from behind her.

"What're you doing here?"

34

Startled by the sound of Lily's voice, Phoenix snapped out of her daze and turned, only to freeze in shock. It was Lily's voice she heard, but it wasn't Lily standing before her. Instead, the person standing before her was a mirror image of herself. A living, breathing doppelganger.

"What the –" Her mouth dropped open as she blinked to clear the illusion. It didn't disappear.

"You're not supposed to be here," the doppelganger said with Lily's voice. "She'll be coming any minute."

Phoenix clasped the sword in front of her and frowned as her brain tried to make sense of what it was seeing. The more she concentrated, the more she could catch a faint trace of Lily's signature, but the image was all wrong.

What the hell is going on?

She was just about to demand answers when the not-quite-Lily rushed towards her, her head swivelling from left to right as if searching for something.

"Lily, why do you look like me?" She took a step back

186

but forced her voice to stay calm to avoid making the young girl more agitated.

"I was going to make it right. You have to believe me."

Desperate hands grasped at Phoenix's sword-free arm and her own wide, green eyes stared pleadingly at her. Alarm bells rang in the deep recesses of her mind, but she couldn't focus past the strange image, or Lily's frantic ramblings, to think straight.

"Lily, calm down. Just tell me what's going on."

"Please, Phoenix, you need to leave. I was wrong. I know that now. I'm sorry. She promised to help me get Annabelle back." Lily's voice broke in a strangled sob. "I just wanted to believe her so badly. But I'm going to fix it. I promise."

A sense of dread wrapped around Phoenix, freezing her to the spot. The hairs on the back of her neck stood to attention, and her hands grew clammy.

Lily abruptly halted her profuse apologising, and her eyes widened into a mask of fear as she stared over Phoenix's left shoulder.

Not one to ignore a warning, Phoenix ducked just in time to miss the blade that sliced through the air where her neck had been less than a second previous. She brought her sword up the meet the follow-through strike and found herself looking into expressionless golden eyes.

The woman wasn't much taller than her, and her body was lean with muscle and a lethal air. Her energy screamed power but had an almost intangible quality that made it hard to identify; just like the first Mist.

"Shit," Phoenix whispered as the woman became a shadow dispersing into the air.

Breath held, she turned in a slow circle, waiting for the

attack she knew to be inevitable.

It came from the left, but not in the form of the Mist herself. Rather, one of the large stones seemed to free itself from the jagged structure to fly at her head.

She only just managed to side-step in time and found herself moving straight into the trajectory of an oddly shaped dagger held by the Mist. The blade sliced through her upper arm and pain blazed in its wake.

Too late to avoid the damage, she continued turning until she was pressed in tight against the Mist. Close enough to make another blade strike difficult, and close enough to look death in the eyes.

She placed her hand against the Mist's chest and called the sun to her. It came more swiftly than ever before and burst from her in a flash of light, but the air beneath her hand was empty. Behind her, Lily screamed, and she turned just in time to see the young witch throw herself in front of the blade that was plunging for her back.

It was all Phoenix could do to yank her backwards, sending them both tumbling to the ground.

The coppery tang of blood filled the air, and Lily's body shimmered beneath her until she was no longer looking at a mirror image of herself but at the true version of Lily. A slight twitch from Lily was enough to assure her the witch was alive. She rolled to her back with the sword still miraculously clutched in her grasp and held it up in a vain attempt to stave off another attack.

But the Mist was gone.

The wind whipped into a frenzy and the sky overhead darkened with oppressive grey clouds. Lightning split the sky, filling the centre of the castle in an eerie white light.

Lily let out a pained groan and rolled to a sitting position beside her. A red stain coated one side of her blue jumper and she clutched her ribs, wincing with each inhale.

"Leave," she pleaded.

"Too late for that," responded a disembodied voice on the wind.

Phoenix jumped to her feet. She turned in a slow circle, sword at the ready, as she stood guard over Lily. Suddenly, sounds berated her from all angles: wordless cries, her name, a language she didn't recognise.

The wind grew in force until it became a visible barrier around her and Lily. Shadows appeared and disappeared, making it impossible to concentrate on a single point. The dizzying sight made her head spin and the world tilted at an odd angle.

A vibration through the hilt of the sword and into her hand shocked her back into focus. Somewhere in the deep recesses of her mind, she heard her father's voice whisper, "Trust your instinct." Words spoken long ago, in another lifetime.

With a deep breath, she let the tension ease from her body and closed her eyes. She fought past all the noise and distraction and tried to centre herself.

Inhale. Exhale.

She raised the sword and sliced through the swirling vortex that surrounded them. There was no resistance, but when she opened her eyes again, the wind was gone, and just as suddenly as it had changed, the sky overhead was cloudless once more.

Atop the northern wall of the castle, the Mist – Maj,

Darius had called her – stood watching her. There was a curious look on her face as she eyed the sword in Phoenix's hand. Something had shifted in the woman's demeanour. It was almost as if her determined stance now held a hint of reluctance.

"Why are you doing this?" Phoenix called, not really expecting the other woman to answer.

For a moment Maj was silent, but then her weary voice carried on the wind. "I have no choice."

Her physical form dissolved to mist once more, and Phoenix braced herself.

The blows came from every angle, invisible but no less painful for their lack of substance. It was all she could do to remain standing. All attempts to block the unseen attacks proved fruitless.

Beside her, Lily stumbled to her feet, hissing in a breath as she attempted to straighten. She pushed the young girl behind her, using herself as a shield as she closed her eyes again. *Focus on the energy,* she reminded herself, and raised the sword before her.

Her next slice met with resistance and a grunt. Then something slammed into the side of her and sent her spinning. She opened her eyes and spun just in time to see the odd-shaped dagger plunging for her chest.

Lily whispered a word Phoenix didn't understand, and time fractured.

The next thing she knew, the witch was standing in front of her, and as she watched, the dagger plunged through Lily's chest. Her body arched back and a scream of agony tore free from her throat.

Phoenix clutched her in disbelief, taking the weight of

her body as it crumpled. She fell to her knees and wrapped her arms tightly around the young girl.

"No, no, no," she demanded, shaking her head as she willed Lily to live with everything she had.

Rage, and pain, and fear, and grief welled up inside her until it felt like she might explode. She squeezed her eyes shut and pushed it all down, but it was too much; she couldn't contain it. The scream ripped from her as all the pain she was feeling combined into the burst of power that exploded from her chest.

Everything went white and her ears rang. It was a few moments before Lily's soft, gasping breaths brought her back to her senses. She opened her eyes, almost expecting to see a large crater surrounding them, but the castle grounds were just as they had been. Minus the Mist.

Lily's body started to shake in her arms and when she looked down, her stomach dropped. The other girl's face was deathly white, and clammy sweat glistened on her forehead. Her body felt so cold. A soft lament drifted on the wind, and panic seized Phoenix.

"It's okay. It's okay. We'll get you help," she said, even as her eyes were drawn to the growing pool of blood surrounding the dagger in Lily's chest.

"I ... I'm sorry ... I was ... I was going to make it right." Lily clutched her hand with surprising strength and gave her a sad smile. "I can be with her now."

The soft lament turned to a keening wail and grew stronger, filling every cell of Phoenix's body. Her grief merged with it, until it was all encompassing, and as Lily's eyes closed for the final time, a single tear broke free.

35

Ethan tapped his foot and mentally willed Nate to drive faster. The flash of light in the distance only meant one thing, and every second it took them to reach Phoenix's side was a second too long.

He'd stubbornly refused to follow her when she stalked out of the house in a huff. She was being completely unreasonable, and truth be told, his whole body felt battered and exhausted as it fought the remnants of poison in his system. He couldn't face yet another fight with her.

Once the anger had worn off, reality filtered back in and he'd started to get antsy at the thought of her out there alone. By that stage, he'd had no way of knowing where she'd gone, and he couldn't find Lily to do a locator spell. Abi had stubbornly refused to help him too, at least until he made her realise the danger Phoenix could be in.

Now, as he saw the castle looming in the horizon, his instincts screamed at him, calling him an idiot of the highest proportions. Adrenaline pushed back the fatigue that still weighed heavy on his body and mind, and he gripped the car's door handle, ready to leap from the moving vehicle as soon as they were close enough.

The car screeched to a halt and he was running, vaguely aware of slamming doors behind him.

He passed the car Phoenix had taken and leapt the low wall. There were no sounds of fighting. There was only an eerie silence, broken by the crunch of soft green grass under his feet as he ran.

Please don't let me be too late.

The jagged edge of the castle wall blocked his view, and it was only when he reached the boundary that he saw them. Phoenix knelt in the grass with a body draped across her lap and sword on the ground by her side. He slowed to a halt as his brain tried to make sense of the scene before him. Was it the Mist? A tourist?

His senses stayed on high alert, fuelled further by the potent energy that enveloped him. Tentatively, he stepped through what had once been a doorway. A soft wind blew in from the coast and it was then he noticed the blonde hair, ruffled by the breeze even as the body lay still. His heart froze.

Phoenix raised her head and turned dull, shocked eyes towards him. A single tear glistened in the fading light of the sun.

His mind struggled to fit the puzzle together, trying valiantly to protect him by offering alternative interpretations. But he knew.

He fell to his knees in the clearing and howled.

Time became inconsequential and Phoenix had no idea how long had passed before the others arrived. She was dimly aware of Ethan's howl of anguish, shortly followed by Abi's gentle sobs and Nate's repeated denials, but she couldn't take her eyes off Lily.

The young girl's face seemed so peaceful now that the lines of tension were finally gone. The flush of colour had left her lips, but there was a softness to them that made it almost seem as if she was smiling, something Phoenix had never seen her do in the short time she'd known her.

But the peaceful image was all wrong. Death shouldn't have been a release for Lily. At eighteen years of age, she should have been full of life and willing to fight with every ounce of her being, not giving it up so readily.

A heavy weariness filled Phoenix and when Nate's haunted eyes appeared in front of her, she let him take Lily. Strong arms wrapped around her and lifted her from the ground. Voices spoke incoherent words, and moments later she was placed gently in the passenger seat of a car. Whose, she had no idea. It didn't matter.

The world blurred past and she let the numbness protect her. But at the back of her mind, a niggling memory was trying to push through to her consciousness.

The box.

She bolted forward only to be jerked back by the seatbelt. The car swerved as, beside her in the driver's seat, Abi jumped at her sudden movement. It was only then that Phoenix looked around the small confines of the car and realised she was alone with her friend.

"Where's Ethan? I need to tell him about the box."

Abi's eyebrows scrunched in confusion and she indicated backwards with her head as she righted the car. "He's behind us with Nate and ..."

Phoenix deflated in the seat as her gut twisted with the remembered sense of foreboding. The dream. The cries for help. Had it been Lily? She should have done more to save her. Somehow, they needed to make sure Lily passed. She needed to be with her sister. The thought caused a fierce burn in the back of Phoenix's throat and she closed her eyes. So much pain. So much death.

They reached the house, followed moments later by the others. Nate carried Lily inside, her body cradled close to his chest, as if he wanted to keep her warm. Before Phoenix could speak to him, Ethan disappeared into the house behind them, his face haggard and drawn.

Abi placed a comforting hand on her shoulder. "Come on. I'll make you tea. It'll help."

Phoenix wasn't sure anything could possibly help at that moment, but she followed obediently. She sat in silence as Abi fussed about the kitchen with determined focus and accepted the steaming cup liberally laced with sugar.

It didn't ease the crushing pain in her chest, but by the time she was finished, she at least felt capable of forming a coherent sentence again. She gave Abi a grateful smile. The smile she got in return didn't reach her friend's blue eyes, and she noted the black circles and bloodshot lines that replaced their usual sparkle. Phoenix added yet another tick to her guilt list before pushing the thought aside; it would help no one.

With a resigned sigh, she stood. "I should go find Ethan and tell him about the box for the Ritual."

Abi gave her a strange look. "He needs you, Phoenix. No matter what he says, don't let him push you away."

Her steps faltered, the words striking a chord in some deep hidden part of herself. She hesitated before nodding, then turned and headed downstairs to find him.

The door to one of the bedrooms was cracked open, and through the narrow gap she could see him sitting on the bed with his head bowed. She knocked tentatively, unsure of her welcome, but when no response came, she slipped into the room anyway.

Ethan didn't look up or acknowledge her, though he had to be aware of her presence. He just stared at his hands, looking utterly lost. The need to comfort him overwhelmed her.

"I was wrong about Shade. I'm so sorry," she admitted softly.

He nodded but didn't look at her.

Abi's words replayed in her head as she hovered uncertainly in the doorway. When, after a minute, he didn't order her to leave, she moved further into the room and sat down on the bed beside him. She could still smell the salty sea air lingering on his skin and an aching sense of loss filled her.

Ethan raised his eyes to hers, and the anguish she saw there mirrored that ache. "It's my fault."

She grabbed his hand and shook her head vehemently. No. She wouldn't let him blame himself for this. "You didn't cause this."

"I didn't stop it either."

"We will."

"What if we don't?"

She shrugged. "Then I guess we'll all end up dead and it won't matter."

His jaw dropped and he stared at her in disbelief. Then suddenly, they both burst out laughing. The kind of hysterical laughter that came when your only other option was to cry. When the laughter finally subsided, she leaned her head on his shoulder. He put an arm around her and pulled her close with a squeeze. His body was warm against hers, solid, and for that moment, the fear faded.

"I think your pep talk needs work."

He pulled away to lift something from the bed behind them. His eyes darkened as he turned back with a white box in his hands. "I think you should see this."

She frowned in confusion, looking from him to the box. The first thing she noticed was the photograph, and her heart spasmed as she recognised Lily's smiling face. Before she could say anything, Ethan lifted the lid and revealed the box's contents.

"I found this in Lily's room."

A solid gold plaque gleamed up at Phoenix, the serpent mocking her from its wooden resting place. Bile rose in her throat and she blinked, her head trying to make sense of what she was seeing.

"Is that –"

"The Ouroboros."

"She had it all along." The words came out in a disbelieving whisper as the truth of what she was looking at hit her.

Tentatively, she reached out to trace the symbol that could have saved her parents. Her skin tingled where she touched the gold, the relic's magic tangible even to her. She pulled her hand back as if burned and clasped it in her lap.

"We don't know that it would have made a difference," Ethan said softly.

The image of her parents stepping into the void flashed into her mind, stealing her breath. Even now she could remember the gut-wrenching pain in that moment of realisation; time hadn't dulled its sharp edge, and she doubted it would ever heal. It was that understanding that brought clarity.

She looked up at Ethan and saw the conflicting emotions warring behind his brown eyes: anger, hurt, betrayal, pain, grief. They'd all experienced so much loss in such a short time, and none of them were really equipped to deal with it. Could she blame Lily for wanting the relic? It was obvious why she'd taken it. If Phoenix had a chance to bring back her loved ones, she'd grab it with both hands.

None of it mattered now. What was done was done.

"It needs to be destroyed," she said finally. "No one else can be allowed to use it."

He nodded and closed the box with a firm click, reminding her of the reason she'd come to find him.

She gave him a sad smile. "I don't have the box for the Ritual. It was burned in the fire."

His eyes searched her face, as if trying to understand what she was feeling. "We'll sort it out, don't worry. We'll make sure she finds Annabelle," he said eventually.

Tears burned at the back of her throat, but she swallowed them. If she let go now, she wasn't sure she'd ever stop. She needed to be strong if she was going to do what had to be done.

"If we can't find an alternative soon, I'm ending this, Ethan. I can't let anyone else die for something I can stop."

He jerked around to face her, his hands grasping her shoulders in a bruising grip. "No!"

The one word was filled with command, but his eyes were desperate and pleading as he dropped his guard and let her see the fear and need hidden under the surface.

And that was her undoing.

His lips found hers, and she hesitated for only a second before she gave in to the firm pressure. The fire was instantaneous as it consumed her. She pressed herself closer, needing the heat of his body against hers. All the while terrified he'd pull away. More terrified he wouldn't.

Her body came alive with sensation, and for once, she let go of the doubt. When he pulled her back with him onto the bed, she didn't resist. She met his need with a hunger of her own, consequences be damned.

36

Darius stalked through the corridor of the Council headquarters, a mask of indifference hiding his deadly intent. Following the Council's decree to confine William, it was decided prudent to keep all Witnesses on site to save on the need for constant portalling. That didn't mesh with his plans, however, and he was damned if he was going to be grounded like a school child while Phoenix ruined centuries of hard work by getting herself killed.

Unfortunately, as much as the Council was full of idiots, they were still powerful idiots, and Diana's barrier spell wasn't one he'd be able to easily break through unnoticed. Which left only one option – he had to kill her.

A sense of anticipation increased his pace and helped to dull the rage their order had sent through him. This was just another test on the path to claiming his rightful station. And truth be told, the witch had it coming to her. Hers was merely a token position on the Council, and the loss would have no great impact; her species was barely a step above humans anyway.

He headed further into the depths of the building, noting a slight downward slope to his trajectory as he moved silently over the marble floor. Each of the Council members had private high security chambers below ground level that were off limits to Witnesses, with only rare exceptions. For the duration of Il Maestro's reign on the Council, Darius had been one of those exceptions, and so he proceeded through the private quarters with a confidence that allowed him to blend into his surroundings.

The sound of low voices drifted from a nearby room, and he slowed his steps. He recognised the voices immediately, but it was only when the conversation grew more heated that they spoke loud enough for the words to become clear.

"Tell us where they'll go," Vlad demanded. "If your loyalty truly lies with the Council, tell us where he'll take the hybrid."

The hybrid? The Council had Phoenix's location; did that mean Maj had failed?

There was a long silence before William responded. "He'll take her to Donegal, to the pack. It's the only thing that makes sense."

"Indeed."

"The pack will stand with him; that's why he'd go there. They won't let you kill her."

"Then they will be destroyed as well."

Vlad's response held no emotion, but Darius could almost feel the satisfaction oozing from him even on the far side of the door. The rumbling growl from William said the werewolf could clearly feel it, too.

Both men stalked out of the room, only to come to an abrupt halt when they saw him.

Vlad barely acknowledged his presence. Instead, he straightened his suit jacket and bid William farewell with a friendly smile that didn't quite reach his eyes before continuing down the corridor. William, on the other hand, narrowed his gaze.

"It seems odd that mere days after we last spoke, the CLO have brought my relationship to the attention of the Council, don't you think?"

Darius inclined his head, but met the man's gaze without flinching. "I appreciate how it must seem, but I assure you that information was held in good faith and passed my lips to none other than you. Unfortunately, it seems Vicktor is a little greyer on the matter of loyalty. With his considerable resources, it's actually surprising it took him this long to discover the connection."

William regarded him closely, his nose twitching subtly as he searched for a lie in the words. "The second Mist failed," he offered eventually.

Darius raised an eyebrow but said nothing.

"Needless to say, the Council is less than happy." William's careful tone made it clear he wasn't including himself in that statement. "Jannah will be sent, the others alongside him. She won't stand a chance. My cousin's pack won't be enough to protect her and my hands are tied."

The words hung heavy in the air, their implication clear. With that, William turned and disappeared down the corridor.

Well, that was a curious turn of events. Phoenix had

managed to evade yet another Mist? She was proving more resourceful than he'd given her credit for.

It wouldn't matter, though. Jannah was one of the most powerful Supes Darius had ever encountered; only the bonds of the Council, and the Mist's own misguided sense of morality, held him in check and prevented Jannah from being a truly terrifying force to reckon with. What a waste.

With a renewed urgency, Darius pulled out his mobile and stepped into the recently vacated office beside him. The phone rang once before being cut off by a robotic answering machine.

"Phoenix," he chastised. "There's really no need to avoid my calls when I'm trying to help you. It seems the Council have reached the limit of their patience. They are sending all three Mists, and they will destroy anyone who chooses to stand with you. My offer of protection still stands. The pack isn't strong enough to survive what you bring to their door, but I am. You have less than twenty-four hours; I suggest you make your decision quickly."

He hung up and immediately called the next number on his list: the Omega.

"Sean, I think it's time you take a little trip home. Just make sure you're not seen. I wouldn't want to have to kill your old pack."

With that task done, he strode out of the office and continued down the corridor. His fangs descended as he walked. He needed a stiff drink.

37

Phoenix kept her gaze firmly on the car ahead of her. Ethan and Nate were leading the way to the pack lands in Donegal and if she lost sight of them, there was every chance she and Abi would end up back in Dublin, given her questionable sense of direction. It was also preferable to focus on something so mundane as the car bumper. Otherwise, she'd be forced to think of the body lying in the back seat of the car.

For a short time, she'd been able to block it all out – the warmth of Ethan's body chasing all thought away – but then she'd gotten Darius's voicemail, and reality had come rushing back so fast it had nearly given her a concussion. Warmth and comfort had been replaced by a chilling sense of fear, and awkward conversations with Ethan had been deferred in favour of strategy meetings with the others.

The general consensus was that they needed to get to the safety of the pack as soon as possible. She couldn't argue with the logic, but a sickening sense of dread had set up camp in her stomach and she couldn't shake the certainty that she was bringing death to Ethan's home.

"Are you nervous?" Abi asked, breaking the weighty silence that filled the car.

Phoenix clutched the steering wheel, trying not to notice the clamminess of her palms. "I don't want anyone to get hurt for me."

"That's not what I meant."

She sighed. She knew exactly what her friend was asking; she just didn't want to think about it. Anyway, meeting Ethan's parents wasn't a big deal. What happened the night before had been a one-off. There was no need to make this into something bigger than it was.

"What if they blame me?" she blurted out, her mouth obviously not on the same wavelength as her head.

"For what?"

She waved vaguely. "For everything. Ethan being hurt. Lily and Annabelle getting killed. Oh, you know, the upcoming apocalypse."

Abi let out a snort of laughter. "Then they'd be idiots. I know there's a big bad prophecy trying to lay all this shit at your feet, but none of this is your fault. Besides, we both know that's not what you're really worried about."

Shrewd blue eyes fixed on her, and Phoenix squirmed. *Not a big deal,* she reminded herself again. *So what if they don't like me?*

Only, it was a big deal. She was going to the pack because of Cormac's offer of protection. Would he rescind that offer when he realised she'd tainted his son? Would she have to look his parents in the eye and face their disgust?

Brake lights glowed from the car ahead. Ethan took a sharp left turn and disappeared between a row of trees.

She followed his lead, holding her breath as she swung into an opening barely wide enough for the car. The suspension shuddered and groaned as they bounced over rough terrain and trees engulfed them. Her teeth rattled as she continued up the winding trail.

After a couple of minutes, they finally emerged from the forest to find themselves surrounded by lush green fields and rolling hills. An occasional dot of colour marked the landscape, hinting at civilisation buried within the untamed wilderness.

"Wow," Abi said on an exhale.

Phoenix stared open-mouthed, her attention split between following Ethan and gawking at the stunning scenery.

As they rounded a bend, a small hill came into view. A glorious house composed equally of brick and glass sat at its peak, looking like something from those designer shows that she'd binge-watched with Abi last summer. Ahead of her, Ethan indicated and turned into a gravelled area at the bottom of the hill before killing the engine. She followed suit and climbed out of the car, still staring in awe at the house.

Ethan grinned and walked over to her. "You like?"

She just nodded, dumbfounded, and his grin widened. He grabbed her hand and tugged her up the path. "Come on. I've a few people I want you to meet."

Suddenly panicked, she turned back to look for Abi. When she spotted her friend lending support to Nate as he gently lifted Lily's body from the car, she sighed and straightened her shoulders, resigned to her fate. If Ethan noticed her reluctance, he didn't comment on it, even though the hand he held was sweating profusely by the time they reached the house.

The front door flung open and a blur of wild brown hair was all Phoenix registered before a woman threw herself, mid-run, at Ethan, breaking the grip he had on her hand. She could hear him laughing as he picked the woman up – not an easy feat considering she was almost as tall as him – and swung her around.

A strange twinge of jealousy stabbed her in the gut, and she crossed her arms around her midsection. It was only when Ethan finally set the woman down and Phoenix got a proper look at her that relief loosened her arms. The face was more feminine, and had significantly less stubble, but the eyes were a mirror image of Ethan's as they assessed her shrewdly.

"Phoenix, this is my twin sister, Sasha. Sash, this is Phoenix."

The other woman tilted her head and looked her up and down. Sasha's expression gave away nothing of her thoughts, so Phoenix did the only thing she could: she met her gaze head on, attempted a friendly smile, and offered her hand, not too sure whether it would be accepted or bitten off.

After a moment, a wide grin broke out on Sasha's face, making her look even more like Ethan, and she shook the offered hand. "Thanks for bringing my big bro home." She pulled him to her side for another hug.

Ethan rolled his eyes but gave her a tight squeeze. "I'm only four minutes older, Sash."

"Four of the most painful minutes of my life," came a voice behind them.

Phoenix turned to see a man and woman walking in their direction. Energy thrummed from them in waves and there was no doubt in her mind that she was about to meet Ethan's parents. She sucked in a breath and subtly wiped her hands on her trousers.

"Mo Faolán." The woman opened her arms and pulled Ethan into a loving embrace.

His mother's hair was long and wild like Sasha's, with only a smattering of grey visible through the rich auburn. At a glance, she could easily have been mistaken for Ethan's sister, if not for the light lines around her brown eyes as she smiled and a calm confidence earned only from life experience.

Ethan returned the embrace for a long moment before breaking away. "Mam, this is Phoenix. Phoenix, my mother, Fia."

Phoenix suddenly found herself enveloped in a hug. Not quite sure how to respond, she patted Fia awkwardly on the back. A small bubble of warmth settled in her chest at the unexpected gesture, and she pulled away with a shy smile.

When she looked at Ethan once more, he was standing straighter and the gentle fondness he'd shown for his mother was now replaced with uncertainty as he faced his father. She held her breath, suddenly uneasy.

"Dad –"

He was stopped in his tracks as his father closed the distance between them and grasped him in a firm embrace. They stayed like that for a moment, and then some manly clearing of throats ensued as the two separated with a slap on the shoulder.

The large open space seemed so much smaller to Phoenix as she took in the combined energy of both men. Ethan's father was a solid wall of muscle. His strong jaw and sombre grey eyes gave him a serious, unyielding air. Like Fia, threads of grey crept from the edges of his hairline and his skin was nicely weathered, but he wore his years well. She could easily imagine him leading the pack. Hell, she almost felt like bowing her head in supplication herself.

"Phoenix." Ethan turned to her. "This is Cormac, my father and Alpha of the Donegal pack."

She gave him what she hoped was a confident smile and held out her hand. He didn't accept it, just looked at her appraisingly. She bristled and squared her shoulders, refusing to flinch from his gaze.

Eventually, he nodded. "You'll do."

He gave her a wink and cheeky smile before wrapping an arm around Fia's shoulders and turning back towards the house.

"Come on, you two. We have things to discuss."

Ethan followed his parents into the cosy sitting room that had been his favourite part of the house growing up. Phoenix trailed in after him, her head swivelling from side to side as she took in his family home. Her gasp made his chest expand with pride.

Floor to ceiling windows formed one corner of the room and revealed the most breath-taking views of the surrounding land. A stone fireplace covered another wall, and oversized grey sofas that begged to be sprawled on filled the space. He managed to restrain himself as they all politely took a seat and faced each other.

"You have a beautiful home." Phoenix earned herself a glowing smile from Fia as she fidgeted beside him.

"Maybe one day you can explore it in less stressful circumstances," Cormac offered, before his steely gaze turned serious once more. "Now, tell me everything."

Ethan had already given him the headlines, but he went through it all again: what they knew of the prophecy, the assassination attempts by the Council, Darius's warning. He could feel the tension radiate from Phoenix with each detail.

"I'm sorry. I should never have come here," she blurted, jumping to her feet.

He grabbed her hand in an attempt to stop her from bolting, but it was his father who responded.

"It's my choice who I offer protection to, lass, and I do so freely." Cormac turned a weighted gaze to Ethan. "The pack, however, must also be free to choose. They'll stand with you, but it must be you that asks it of them. I won't do it for you."

He'd expected his father to say as much, but his stomach still tightened with the implication of the words. The thought of facing the pack after everything that had happened ... It would be so much easier to just leave and face the Mists alone, but that would be the coward's way out. And probably death.

He looked at Phoenix, the warmth of her hand seeping through his skin. He nodded.

No more running.

It didn't take long for the arrangements to be made, and within half an hour, the entire pack was gathered outside the house. Ethan stood before them, at his father's side for the first time since he'd left – for the first time since Sean's death – and he felt the weight of every eye on him.

From the moment he was born, he'd been taught the responsibility of an Alpha, but only now did he truly understand it. Only now did he acknowledge the fear that responsibility brought, and the real reason he'd run away.

Nervous energy thrummed from Phoenix as she stood behind him with Nate and Abi, and it was that alone that gave him the strength to stand tall and step forward – he needed to be strong for her.

"I've missed you all." He looked at the faces that had surrounded him since childhood, and his wolf sighed contently as the pack's energy wrapped itself around and through him. "My wolf has yearned to run with you again, but I denied it out of fear. I failed this pack by running away, and I failed Sean, our Omega, when he tried to help me. The thought of failing more of you terrifies me."

He let the admission hang in the air, waiting for them to turn from him or look away in disgust. They didn't.

"I've come to ask something very dangerous of you, and I know I don't deserve to. But there's something coming that's bigger than all of us, and if we don't find a way to face our fears now, many people will suffer. The Council is coming for this woman" – he pointed to Phoenix – "because of a prophecy she has no part in. One she's actively trying to stop. They want to keep this secret from the Lore and they're sending the Mists.

"It's likely they will kill anyone who tries to protect her, Supe or human alike. They've already tried, and failed, three times. I intend to see to it that they fail for a final time. And I'm asking you to stand with me. My family has pledged their protection, and you are free to make your own choice. But our strength comes from the pack. So I'm asking you, will you lend us your strength now?"

A heavy silence hung in the air, and Ethan held completely still, his breath frozen in his chest.

"The Alpha said you killed the vamp that murdered Sean. Is that true?" A woman stepped forward through a break in the crowd and he immediately recognised the gentle features of Sean's mother.

He inclined his head. "I'm sorry I couldn't do it for you sooner, Sarah."

She nodded her acknowledgement and squared her shoulders, standing tall and sure. "I will stand with you against the Council and in all future battles to come."

Low murmurs filled the crowd, and her words were echoed by male and female voices alike. One by one, the wolves of the Donegal pack bent to one knee around him, offering their pledge.

38

Phoenix bit her lip as she stared at the map that was rolled out over the kitchen table. The pack lands were substantial, with many of the wolves residing within the dotted boundary Cormac had marked. A large community building sat at the centre surrounded by woodlands, and they all agreed this was the best place to make their stand.

"And you're sure the Mists can't just appear wherever they like?" she asked, her stomach twisting into an uncomfortable knot.

Cormac gave her a grim smile. "As sure as I can be, lass. The entire boundary was warded by the local coven to prevent access to anyone we don't want in. But once they break the ward – and they will – there won't be any restriction on their magic."

Her palms turned sweaty, and she glanced at Ethan before letting her gaze rest on Abi, who stood against the wall listening intently to their every word.

"How do we keep everyone safe?"

"By doing the best we can." Fia gave her a compassionate smile from the far side of the table, but her eyes were hard, determined. "There are wolves monitoring the perimeter, and the rest of us will meet at the community centre to prepare. But first, I think there's something we need to do?"

Phoenix looked towards Nate. He'd been unusually quiet throughout the discussion and though he appeared to be listening, his lack of contribution worried her. He was the strategy guy; he should be in his element now, but he just seemed pensive and distant. Maybe once they conducted the Ritual, it would help him focus. They could all fall apart later – if they survived.

She nodded in response to Fia's question. "Do you have what we need?"

Ethan held up a small box wrapped with white rope. "Everything's set up and ready to go. I didn't know how much time we'd have and I wanted to make sure ..."

She reached out and squeezed his hand, swallowing past the lump in her throat as she prepared herself for yet another goodbye.

One by one, they filed out of the house and headed for the woods. Only Nate remained behind, promising to follow in a few moments. They didn't have to walk far before they came to a small clearing illuminated by the sliver of moon that hung low in the sky. Lush grass dotted with beautiful white flowers covered the area. Energy filled the space, not quite as strong as the Cathedral, but similar.

"The clearing is blessed so that we can help pack members pass," Ethan said quietly, his shoulder brushing against hers as he came to a stop by her side.

Before she could say anything, a rustle drew her attention back to the trees and Nate stepped into view with Lily cradled in his arms. He kept his head bowed, his messy hair obscuring his eyes as he moved to the centre and laid her down.

In her hands, he placed a faded photograph Phoenix had never seen before. Two smiling girls stared up at her from the picture, so full of life and potential that would never be realised. She balled her own hands into fists and focused on the sting of her nails digging into her palms.

Silently, Nate prepared the herbs, shaking his head when Ethan moved to help him. When he was done, he closed his eyes for a moment, then stepped back to join the rest of them in forming a circle around Lily. Wolves of all colours and sizes appeared in the shadows of the trees, and even without a connection to the pack, Phoenix could feel their offer of strength as they stood together in solidarity.

The air grew heavy as Nate spoke the words that were now all too familiar to her. A soft lament, different from the keening she'd heard at the castle, or at any of the other Rituals, floated on the wind. The sound was gentle and filled with sorrow, but also hope. Warmth flooded her chest and energy danced over her skin like static electricity.

The words grew in power and the wind picked up in force, whipping her hair across her face. As Lily's body turned to dust on the wind, the wolves raised their heads to the sky and howled. Their song mingled with the lament only she could hear.

It was then that the large black wolf caught her eye. Its strange red eyes stared knowingly at her from across the clearing. There was something so familiar about those eyes, but the knowledge floated just out of her mind's reach.

She blinked, only to find a pale woman with long black hair and an unreadable expression where the wolf had been. They stared at each for what seemed like an eternity before the woman nodded and disappeared, replaced by a large black crow with those same familiar red eyes.

The lament ended and the wind calmed. The centre of the clearing was now empty of everything except the photograph. Phoenix stared at it in confusion, then looked back towards the crow, but that, too, was gone. A sense of calm settled over her, and somehow she knew that Lily was finally at peace.

"You okay?" Ethan asked quietly.

She sighed, her eyes doing one final sweep of their surroundings for any sign of the crow. "We've had to do far too many of these Rituals."

He smiled sadly. "Let's hope it's the last. Guess we should start getting everyone –"

All around her, the wolves froze.

She looked at Ethan and her breath caught. Even before Cormac said the words, she knew.

"They're here."

39

Ethan stared at Phoenix, memorising every line on her face. Her panicked eyes met his and he swore to himself then and there that she'd survive this, even if it meant giving his own life. With effort, he tore his gaze away and turned to his father.

"We need to get everyone to the community centre before they break the wards."

Cormac gave a short nod and set about issuing orders for the wolves to prepare. The telepathic link he held to the pack allowed him to give the rest of the wolves fair warning of what was to come. But were any of them truly ready?

Phoenix grabbed him by the arm. "Where's Nate? He's meant to protect Abi."

Sure enough, when Ethan looked around, there was no sign of the shifter. The photograph that Nate had placed with Lily's body had also disappeared. He cursed under his breath.

"I can fight." Abi stood behind Phoenix, her head held high even as her voice trembled slightly. "Nate has been teaching me, and I have some protection charms Lily made me ..."

He gave her a reassuring smile and squeezed Phoenix's shoulder. "I don't doubt that you'd give half the people here a run for their money, but let's get you back to the community centre first."

As if reading his mind, Sasha appeared at his side. "I can go with Abi. She can keep me safe." She winked at the other girl, and he smiled gratefully at his sister for helping to ease the tension.

In the back of his mind, he could hear the buzz from the pack, and it was only with effort that he managed to block it out enough to focus. If the tightness in his father's posture was anything to go by, they didn't have much time left.

There were no explosions or flashes of light as the Mists worked against the wards. In fact, the night was eerily silent. But when Cormac went deathly still, Ethan knew.

A howl filled the night, only to be abruptly cut off.

"They're through," Fia whispered.

"Go!" Ethan ordered, shoving Sasha and Abi towards the trees.

All around him, wolves leapt into action, turning the clearing into a chaos of activity as everyone hurried to safety. Within seconds, only Cormac, Fia, and Phoenix remained with him.

"We need to buy them time." He looked at Phoenix and bit his tongue to hold back the order for her to leave; it was obvious from the stubborn set of her shoulders that she was staying whether he liked it or not.

"If we spread out along the perimeter, we can hold

them off in the woods," Cormac said, his gaze distant as he mentally monitored the movements of the pack.

Ethan turned to Fia. "Okay, dad and I will take the eastern side. You and Phoenix take the western side." He allowed the unspoken plea to show in his eyes: keep her safe for me.

His mother grabbed him in a fierce hug, then pulled Phoenix into the trees with her, not giving him a chance to say anything further. A steely-eyed nod from his dad was the only acknowledgement before he, too, disappeared into the darkness.

Ethan stood alone in the clearing. He allowed himself only a second to focus his mind, then he was off, running through the woods to face death head on.

He'd barely cleared the treeline when the screeches started. He skidded to a halt. Birds, humans, animals, their cries echoed and faded like ghosts on the wind. The utter terror caused his every nerve ending to thrum.

They need help.

He swivelled his head, frantically trying to pinpoint the direction, but their pain and torment was everywhere.

Then his name, a cry for help. His own terror mirrored that of the screaming voices.

Phoenix.

He set off at a run again, crashing through the trees in a blind panic. But it didn't matter which way he turned; her calls always came from behind him, always out of reach.

Flashes of lightning hit the four corners of the compass and filled his vision with blotches of white light. He stumbled on blindly, his hands clawing at branches as they tangled around him.

Ethan!

Cormac's voice broke through the fog in his mind, and instantly his wolf calmed. He slid to a stop with his hand on a large oak tree and forced his breathing to slow. He closed his eyes and let his wolf's instincts take over.

The cries for help stopped, and the night fell silent except for the rustle of leaves in the gentle breeze. The illusion faded away, and he felt the tug in the centre of his chest as the pack link pulled him back to reality and grounded him.

"Impressive." Shayan's familiar voice drifted on the wind.

The hairs on the back of Ethan's neck stood to attention and a throbbing pain filled his chest. He turned in a slow circle, extending his claws as he did. He was going to make this hurt.

Shadows wove between the trees, teasing their way towards him only to retreat again. He stayed completely still and waited.

"I thought you'd be dead by now," the disembodied voice mused.

Memories bombarded Ethan: a fist plunging into his chest. Excruciating pain. Never-ending darkness. "I thought the Council would have killed you for your failure," he ground out.

A burst of lightning struck the tree next to him, and he grinned. *Guess that hit a nerve.*

"We won't fail this time."

With that, the screeching came again, even louder than before. Ethan fell to his knees, hands over his ears as the piercing noise battered his ear drums. It was no use; the sound infiltrated his mind, growing so loud he was sure his head would explode.

He grabbed for the place deep in the core of his being that tethered him to the pack and bared his teeth. But it was the image of Phoenix that forced him back to his feet, one painstaking step at a time.

The shadows coalesced, swirling together to take the form of a man. Shayan stood before him, tanned skin now marred with healing burn patches. His golden eyes were expressionless despite the cocky smile on his face. He held his palms open and began to speak softly, the energy building around him.

Suddenly, he stopped. His head tilted as if listening to something in the distance.

Ethan's instincts roared to life and he fought to hear past the shrieking that filled his head. When Shayan turned a satisfied smile in his direction, he knew – Phoenix was near.

With a wink, the Mist disappeared and heavy fog descended over the forest.

Ethan ran. The only clear thought in his mind was to save her.

The fog was so thick he could barely see two feet in front of his face. With it came an unnatural silence that was almost louder than the previous screeching. He let his wolf guide him through the trees, trusting the instincts of the beast more than those of the man.

He tried desperately to reach his mother through the

pack link, to warn her Shayan was coming, but it was as if the fog had coated him in a blanket and blocked him off from the outside world.

After what seemed like an eternity, he broke the tree-line, only to find himself back in the clearing where they'd started. Shayan stood in the centre with Fia snarling at him on one side and Phoenix looking equally as feral on the other. Both were poised to attack, but the Mist appeared unconcerned.

Not breaking his stride, Ethan barrelled into Shayan from behind. The Mist stumbled but quickly regained his footing.

With a single word, Ethan was flung sideways against a tree.

Fia and Phoenix took that moment to attack, their movements lethal and beautiful to behold.

It gave him the split second he needed to climb to his feet, but before he could do anything to help, spidery tendrils of shadow slipped from the trees and combined to form a woman.

She wore similar robes to Shayan and her tanned skin was also mapped with raw, red burn marks, hers significantly fresher. Her golden eyes assessed him with cold calculation before she once more disappeared.

The first slash of the dagger came from his left, the gleaming blade aimed for his throat. He stumbled away and sliced upward with his claws, only to meet air.

Her next attack was lower and from the right, intent on gutting him. His quick side-step limited the damage to a superficial slice, but again, she disappeared before he could retaliate. He growled in frustration.

Luck and instinct afforded him a minor win when she rematerialized in front of him just in time to meet the slash of his claws.

It didn't stop the dagger in her hand from plunging into his side, however. Or the solid roundhouse she sent to his knee, causing his leg to buckle with a sickening crunch.

Maj stood over him, seemingly oblivious to the blood soaking her chest, and raised her hands to the sky. Lightning illuminated the night and coalesced into a ball of blue light surrounding her hands. She looked back at him, her golden eyes glowing, and he knew he was well and truly fucked.

The air crackled with building power and somewhere in the distance, he could hear Phoenix scream his name. Ethan braced himself.

A loud growl came from the forest and before Maj could focus her energy, a huge white wolf rammed into her side. Teeth and claws attacked her unrelentingly, driving her back.

She flung the blue ball of light at the wolf, scorching its side and filling the air with the smell of burnt flesh. The wolf simply bared its teeth and leapt for her, its powerful jaws locking around her forearm in a vice grip.

Pain tightened Maj's features, but she didn't cry out. With what seemed like effort, she faded to shadow and dispersed on the heavy fog.

The wolf stood panting for a moment, then turned to look at him, blue eyes filled with an intelligence and familiarity that stopped his heart.

He'd only ever known one wolf to look like the one before him. That wolf was dead.

Ethan gritted his teeth and pushed up to standing, all of his weight on the right leg. Tentatively, he stretched out a hand, convinced what he was seeing had to be an illusion. But before he could reach the snow-white fur, the wolf turned and bolted into the forest.

The sounds of fighting filled his ears and everything pulled back into sharp focus. He turned back towards his mother and Phoenix just in time to see Cormac break through the trees on the far side of the clearing.

Shayan evaded a strike from Fia and pivoted to take in the scene. Three wolves and one pissed off hybrid stood before him. Obviously not favouring the odds, he disappeared in a blink, leaving them all staring at each other warily.

40

Phoenix was panting hard by the time they reached the edge of the forest. The heavy fog that pervaded the air made it difficult to breathe, and her lungs burned with each inhale. As soon as they stepped from the trees, however, the fog disappeared, leaving only a calm night sky and a pensive silence.

Miraculously, their path back to the community centre had been unimpeded, and she couldn't help the healthy dose of wariness that kept adrenaline roaring through her veins. The four of them alone shouldn't have been sufficient to deter a follow-up attack from the Mists, especially not if all three were present.

The community centre lay before them in the middle of a field the size of a football pitch. That open space was all that stood between them and backup, and it was enough to make her want to piss her pants.

Ethan hobbled up beside her, and she got her first clear look at him without the fog blurring her vision. Blood coated his side, and he was purposely keeping his weight off his left leg. A vague expression of shock lingered on his unnaturally pale face even as his eyes scoured their surroundings for any sense of threat.

She let Fia and Cormac move ahead of them and offered him a shoulder to lean on. Her concern only increased further when he took it without complaint.

"You okay?"

"I saw something in the forest ... I ..." He shook his head. "It doesn't matter. Let's just get through this."

They moved quickly. As soon as they were in sight of the community centre, the doors flung wide. Sasha and Abi urged them forward before slamming the doors closed behind them. Locks clicked into place, and Phoenix blinked from the glare of the fluorescent lights.

She was dimly aware of Ethan's weight leaving her shoulders as Sasha slipped her arm around him and hurried away. Fia and Cormac conferred quietly between themselves before disappearing down the stark corridor towards the auditorium. Abi linked her arm and tugged her in the same direction, their footsteps echoing around them.

"What's the plan?"

Phoenix stopped at the entry to the auditorium, a heavy weariness settling in her heart. She grabbed Abi's hands in her own and looked her friend in the eye.

"The plan is I need you to hide." She shook her head to stop the protest that was visibly forming on Abi's lips. "Please, I need you to do this for me. The Mists are coming, and when they get here, I won't be able to protect you."

"It's not your job to protect me."

"I'm the reason you're mixed up in this shit. So yes, it bloody well is." She choked back the fear that threatened to drown her and pleaded, "People are going to die tonight, Abi. Innocent people. I need you not to be one of them."

Worry, fear, and sadness clouded her friend's features as she bit her lip and nodded. The tears that settled along the rim of her blue eyes were stubbornly held back, and when Sasha returned indicating it was time to go, Abi didn't protest. She also didn't say goodbye.

With a shaky breath, Phoenix walked into the auditorium to join the rest of the wolves. Most were in full wolf form, their strongest and most resilient form, with only the higher-ranking werewolves staying human. Cormac and Fia were busy organising everyone, but she paid little attention; she already knew the plan. Instead, she looked around the large open space and memorised every person and wolf that stood in the room with her.

How many of them would die tonight? They were risking their lives to protect her. Without question. If she somehow managed to survive this night, they'd have her undying loyalty.

She felt the comforting warmth of Ethan's presence behind her even before his hand touched her lower back.

"You ready?"

She closed her eyes and took a deep breath, inhaling his familiar scent. The copper tang of blood mingled with the earthiness of the forest that lingered on his skin. His knee was now strapped for support and the worst of the blood had been cleaned from his side, but his face was still drawn and she knew in her heart he wasn't at full strength.

An ache of sadness settled in her chest and she pushed it back resolutely. She reached out for his hand and nodded.

Suddenly, a loud explosion filled the night.

The ground shook beneath Phoenix's feet, and she grabbed Ethan's arm to steady herself. Plasterboard cracked from the ceiling and dust rained down on them, sending her into a coughing fit.

"Looks like they heard us," Ethan said with a wry grin.

Snarling wolves raced past them, ready for the fight that awaited. With one last look at Ethan, she turned and followed.

The ground crumbled beneath her feet as she ran, and she only just managed to avoid a huge crevice that appeared out of nowhere, leaping over it to grasp the doorway for balance.

She expected to hear the sound of fighting from the night beyond, but the only thing that reached her was the angry growls of the wolves. Carefully, she slipped through the door to assess the scene.

The three Mists stood in the middle of the field, unmoving. Two of the three were painfully familiar to her; the third was a man she'd never seen before. He stood ahead of the other two, and an aura of immense power surrounded him as his black robes flowed around his body. His palms were held out to the side and, even in the weighty dark of the night, she could see the glow from his golden eyes. She shivered.

All across the front of the building, the wolves formed a terrifying wall of teeth and claws. They snarled and strained, but seemed unable to move forward. She glanced in confusion at Ethan as he slipped through the door behind her. A raised eyebrow was his only response.

Crouching down, she moved forward, only to hit an

invisible barrier. A low growl from Ethan confirmed the same on his side – the Mists had them trapped.

Lightning struck the ground mere feet to her left. A yelp of pain was accompanied by the sickening stench of burnt flesh, and Ethan roared in fury.

"Fucking cowards. Face us with honour." He rammed his shoulder against the barrier, but it didn't budge. And neither did the Mists.

"How do we fight them if we can't reach them?" She looked around in panic, expecting another bolt of lightning at any second.

The ground beneath their feet rumbled, and she widened her stance in an attempt to keep her balance. The air was heavy, charged with the promise of death; they were sitting ducks.

Ethan grabbed her shoulder and turned her to him. "You can reach them."

His expression was one of unquestioning confidence. She didn't share his faith in her ability, but when his hand grasped hers, she took a deep breath and closed her eyes. She had to try.

Ethan began issuing orders to the wolves to get ready. She blocked it all out and focused only on the heat simmering in the centre of her chest, waiting to be called. Magic filled the air, and she knew they were out of time. She held the image of the Mists in her mind and let go.

The burst of light was so bright that it seared itself into her retinas, causing colours to dance like a bad trip in front of her eyes. For a moment, everything seemed to move in slow motion, almost like the aftermath of a bomb blast. Then the heat wave exploded outward.

The invisible barrier shattered, and the wolves surged forward.

Everything turned into a blur of movement. Wolves leapt through the air only to have their targets disappear on contact.

The Mists blinked out of existence and reappeared a hundred strong. Their illusion was so powerful, it was impossible to tell apparitions from reality.

Phoenix searched for an opening that would allow her to make further use of her powers without hurting her allies, but it was complete chaos.

The night filled with the same screeching they'd heard in the forest. A number of the wolves fell to the ground, howling in pain, while even more turned on each other, unable to recognise friend from foe in their disorientated state.

The air shimmered to her right and Shayan materialised, his once cocky grin now a grimace of burn-tightened skin. Before he could move in her direction, Fia stepped between them, teeth bared and eyes blazing.

"You hurt my son."

She dived at him in a ferocious blur of slashing claws that made Phoenix's jaw drop. Ethan moved to help, but the air solidified in front of him to reveal Maj, holding the very same dagger that had killed Lily. He growled and lunged for her.

Once more, Phoenix tried to call on her power, but before she could, the third Mist stepped in front of her. She stood frozen to the spot as Jannah's golden eyes pulled her into their molten depths. Dimly, she knew she should be afraid; he was here to kill her.

"Don't worry. I'll make it a quick death for them," he promised solemnly.

A voice inside her head screamed for her to fight, but a heavy lethargy fell over her. Her limbs were leaden and her eyelids blinked closed. She forced them back open with effort.

"They don't deserve to die. *We* don't deserve to die."

He gave her a sad smile and raised his hand. A golden light flared in his palm. It called to her, beckoning her forward.

In a distant part of her mind, she heard Cormac shout her name. Then, suddenly, he was there. He shoved her sideways, breaking the hold Jannah had on her mind. The golden ball of energy that had been meant for her skimmed the side of his body, and he tumbled to the ground.

His roar of pain pulled her back to the scene around her, and she stared in horror. Wolves littered the field, bloody and wounded. Those still standing appeared to be battling a vast array of monsters that flitted in and out of existence; illusions, but no less deadly for being so.

So much blood. So much sacrifice.

Her heart wept and every cell in her body screamed for her to protect them. Time fractured in that moment, and when, out of the corner of her eye, she saw Ethan fall to his knees in front of Maj, something inside her shattered.

Rage flooded through her and her body started to shake as a fierce pressure built in her solar plexus. She dropped to her knees and placed her hands on the cold, hard earth beneath her. She called to the sun, and it came.

Grass burst into flames and a ring of white-hot fire surrounded her. Jannah stood watching her on the far side, his eyes mirroring the flames back to her in an almost hypnotic way.

She focused as hard as she could, willing the fire to spread until it formed a barrier around the wolves closest to her. Many were caged in with the illusions they faced, but no further attack would reach them.

Still she pushed further, ignoring the skull-splitting headache that flared to life as she did. There were so many. She needed to protect them.

Through the flame, Jannah looked at her with something akin to respect. "I want you to know I take no pleasure in this."

Phoenix gritted her teeth as her vision turned black.

41

The darkness surrounded Phoenix and threatened to drown her. She was dimly aware of Ethan yelling her name, and she clung to the sound of his voice like a lifeline. But she couldn't hold the power she'd created. Her energy faded and the flames winked out of existence, leaving only scorched earth.

Through her hazy vision, she saw Jannah raise his hands to the sky. His lips moved, forming the unintelligible words that she knew would seal her fate. With gritted teeth, she forced herself to her feet; if she was going to die, she'd bloody well do it standing, not cowering on the ground. She swayed unsteadily.

A blur of movement from the forest caught her attention, and a hysterical laugh bubbled up in her chest as she imagined she saw faces flitting among the shadows. Was this it? Had her mind finally cracked now that she faced the end?

The energy coming from Jannah was so powerful that it was getting difficult to breathe. It pressed against her sternum with a crushing force and she knew that when he let it go, nothing would remain. She closed her eyes and a single tear burned a path down her cheek. That one tear for everything that would never be.

She welcomed the pressure that enveloped her, let it merge with her essence, and she focused on one simple thought: I have to save them.

The realisation brought with it an instant calm. She let the heat build inside her until it felt like she might burn from the inside out. Jannah's power pushed back against it, trying to crush her. Her flames lapped hungrily at the edges of his power, ready to break free, ready to burn.

She would die tonight. But so would he.

Her eyes snapped open and she looked at the Mist. The image that reflected back at her from his golden pupils was full of fury and fire. The nod he gave her was one of acceptance.

She could hear shouts of confusion from all around her, but she had only one goal in mind now.

The power continued to grow inside her until sweat ran in rivulets down her spine. She took a step towards him, her head feeling like it might explode as his energy enveloped her. Then another step. He reached out a hand to her, and she took it, surprised at the softness of his skin.

A blur of movement and a glint of gold were the only things that registered in her mind before Shade magically materialised beside Jannah with another man at his side. They flung a large chain-link sheet of gold over the Mist, and instantly the energy holding her weakened.

Strong arms wrapped around her waist and pulled her backwards. She landed in a heap on the ground. Ethan's "humph" in her ear snapped her out of the trance she'd been in.

The field was full of men and women she didn't recognise. She could tell by their signatures that they were vampires, but her mind struggled to make sense of much more than that.

Two large groups surrounded Shayan and Maj, Fia standing guard with one, and an injured Cormac with the other. Both Mists had similar sheets of gold chain covering them, and though their magic lingered in the air, she could see no sign of their illusions, and neither of them were struggling.

"I don't know how long the gold will hold them." The blonde vampire with Shade offered his hand to help her up from the ground.

The English accent took her by surprise, and she eyed him warily. The vamp appeared to be in his forties, and his grey eyes were kind but serious. She'd never seen his face before, but for some reason she was certain he wasn't one of Darius's vamps. A quick glance around her found no familiar faces from her time living in the Dublin vampire lair. Who were these people?

Before taking the offered hand, she looked in askance to Shade. At his nod, she accepted the help and got, not so gracefully, to her feet. As she did, she reached back to pull Ethan up behind her.

He hissed, yanking his hand away, and she glanced at him in surprise. It was only when she saw him gripping a raw red hand that she realised she'd burned him with her touch; the power of the sun still vibrating through her body.

A quick look at the blonde vampire revealed a similar burn on the hand he'd offered, yet his face showed no sign of anger or pain.

"Who are you?"

"My name is Lucas. I'm your father's Sire."

She sucked in a breath, expecting any answer but that. What did she say to the man who had turned his back on her dad?

"And these ..." She gestured to the field where the other vampires were helping the injured wolves.

"Are your father's clan."

"Were!" She glared at him, daring him to contradict her. Her father hadn't spoken of his past much, but she knew the scars his banishment had left; they were a shadow forever lurking behind his loving gaze.

Lucas gave her a sad smile and nodded in acknowledgement of her words.

Shade cleared his throat. "Not to break up the family reunion, but we still have a situation to deal with."

As one, they turned to Jannah, who was watching them with a blank expression.

Phoenix wrapped her arms around her midsection. Ethan moved to her side and she flinched, afraid of burning him again.

He nudged her with a playful grin and when his skin didn't start to sizzle, he draped an arm over her shoulder, leaning on her for support.

"If we release them, they'll never stop hunting you," Lucas said softly.

The words chilled her, and she pressed closer to Ethan's side. "I'm not a killer."

"Neither are we when we have a choice." There was no pleading in Jannah's tone, simply truth.

She assessed the Mist for a moment, then moved towards him, ignoring Ethan's attempt to hold her back. "But you won't stop."

His golden eyes darkened with unspoken pain and he shook his head. "We're bound by our debt to the Council. So long as they control us, we have no choice."

Her eyes fell on the thick golden bands encasing his wrists and the clenched fists beneath. The thin golden chain-link sheet glinted in the moonlight; it had been enough to nullify the Mists' magic. What were those thick bands capable of?

Lucas stepped up beside her, his eyes flicking to the bands as well. "What if you had a choice?"

42

The plan was simple, Lucas explained. Release the Mists from the threat of their golden bonds by using lead – gold's magical opposite – to weaken the structural integrity enough to break them. Phoenix listened, but the logic was lost on her.

If it was really that simple, why hadn't the Mists broken free long before now? She asked as much, directing her question to Jannah, who'd remained silent as Lucas spoke.

"The vampire is right. If the bonds can be broken, we'd be free of the Council control," the Mist answered, his expression grave. "The problem isn't the bonds, however; it's the spell protecting us from them. It is only our obedience that stops the spell from releasing, and once it does, the gold comes into contact with our skin."

His tone implied dire consequences, and Phoenix looked closely at him, suddenly aware that he'd barely moved at all since the chain-link had been thrown over him. If anything, his posture seemed to have withered, almost imperceptibly. A quick look at the other two Mists showed an even more obvious weakening. If that was the reaction to such a thin sheet of gold, what would the thick bands around their wrists do?

"How bad?" she asked, turning her attention back to him.

"A minute, maybe less, before the gold drains our life force completely."

She sucked in a breath.

"It can be done. We just need to be quick." Lucas gave her a confident smile that made her stomach drop.

"How exactly are you going to combine the gold and lead?" She didn't want to know the answer. She really didn't.

"I'm not. You are."

She shook her head and backed away with her hands held up. "Oh no. No way. I'd burn them to a crisp."

He shrugged. "That's the chance they'll take." With a wave of his hand, two vampires appeared beside them with Cormac, Fia, and the other two Mists in tow. "The only question is whether or not you're willing to try."

Her jaw dropped; he was actually serious. This was insane. The three people standing in front of her had each tried to kill her. One had almost killed Ethan, and another had succeeded in killing Lily.

As if reading her thoughts, Maj met her gaze square on. "You would be within your rights to take this opportunity for vengeance. In your position, I'm not sure I would do anything else."

Phoenix looked into the eyes of the woman that had killed a young girl and saw a shadow of regret. She also saw something else: steel. The Mist would accept her fate with honour.

"You hesitated. Back at the castle. Why?"

A small smile lifted the corner of Maj's mouth, but it didn't reach her eyes. "I didn't relish the death of potential."

The cryptic words just caused Phoenix's head to ache even more. She sighed wearily.

"I'm not a murderer, despite what the Council may have you believe. I won't kill you while you're unable to defend yourself."

A look of surprise flashed momentarily across the Mists' face, and Maj nodded in acknowledgement of the uneasy truce.

At her side, Phoenix could feel the tension emanating from Ethan. His jaw clenched tight and his eyes blazed as he stared at the woman that had killed Lily. He put his hand on her lower back and spoke close to her ear. "You don't have to do this."

A large part of her wanted to grasp the offered out with both hands, but that was the cowardly part of her. That part of her wanted the Mists gone, and for this to be all over, but it wasn't that simple.

She stepped forward, fists clenched to stop her hands from trembling. "If I do this, I want your blood vow that you will never harm anyone here again."

Something dark and terrifying swirled in the depths of Jannah's golden eyes. "If you can free us from the Council's control, you will have more than that," he promised. "You will have our vow to stand at your side when the time comes."

She shivered as a strange fluttering filled her stomach.

And so it was agreed. Lucas placed two small pieces of lead in her hand, then produced a dagger and extracted the blood oath from Jannah.

The moment he uttered the oath, the spell protecting him from his bonds released, and he fell to his knees with a pained cry.

Phoenix was so surprised by the reaction that she fumbled with the lead and dropped it on the ground. She scrambled to pick it up and turned to kneel before him.

Sweat coated his paling skin and his face contracted in agony. The effort it took him to lift his wrists left her in no doubt that she was working on limited time.

With shaking hands, she raised the two pieces of lead until they were under his wrists. "Ready?"

She took his grunt as confirmation and closed her eyes. It didn't take much to heat the lead in her hands, and strangely, it didn't hurt. The scary part came when she had to control her energy enough not to barbecue the Mist on contact.

Slowly, she inched her hands upwards, her heart in her mouth as she closed the gap between the lead and the gold. There was no resistance, and the stench of crispy-fried flesh never came. She opened her eyes in surprise.

Jannah's wrists rested in her palms, and the bonds surrounding them were now a strange swirling mix of lead and gold. He raised his head and stared at them in awe. His golden eyes glowed and the air grew heavy with the weight of his magic.

The words he whispered were weak, but they danced across her skin as if they had physical substance. His form shimmered in a soft golden glow, and his bonds cracked in half and fell to the ground with a loud thud.

There was no rejoicing, or even a show of emotion at his newfound freedom. He simply closed his eyes for a moment before turning to Maj and Shayan. "I'll help you block it as best I can."

So, two more blood oaths were taken, and two more Mists were freed of their bonds. By the end, Jannah was so weak from his attempts to shield his siblings from the gold that Shayan and Maj had to support him on either side to simply keep him upright.

Shayan gave her an assessing look, no cockiness evident in his gaze now. "The Council won't stop. You know that, don't you?"

Nate's unexpected voice answered from behind her. "That's where I come in."

Ethan led Phoenix, Shade, and Nate back to his parent's house while the others stayed behind to tend to the wounded pack members. Adrenaline roared through his veins, unspent and in need of release. They had come so close to losing everything.

"Where the hell have you been?" he yelled at Nate as soon as the front door closed behind them.

The shifter held his laptop up defensively in front of him. "Let me show you before you eat me."

Ethan bared his teeth as Nate pushed past, but followed him to the kitchen, nonetheless. Maps from their earlier planning were strewn across the large table, and half empty cups of tea sat waiting for their owner's return.

Nate placed the laptop on top of the maps, and his fingers danced over the keyboard. The screen went black for a second before green writing started scrolling along the bottom like a breaking news bulletin.

A few of the words in particular jumped out at Ethan: hybrid, Lore, prophecy, Council, murder.

"What am I looking at?"

Phoenix leaned past him for a closer look, and his frustration was momentarily forgotten as he watched her face scrunch in concentration. How close had he come to losing her tonight? His chest constricted at the thought.

"It took me longer than I hoped to hack into the Council's security network, which is why Shade went to get us more help." Nate held up a hand to stall any questions. "I only managed to get in just before the Ritual, and by then it was too late to tell you our plan. The feed you're looking at is currently the only thing running on their operating systems and can be broadcast worldwide on all forms of human media with the push of a button."

Beside Ethan, Phoenix gasped, mirroring his own surprise. "You're going to expose the Lore?"

Nate gave them his trademark cheeky grin – the first Ethan had seen in a while.

"Of course not. That would be suicide. We just need them to think we are."

The cogs were turning slowly in Ethan's head. His body still hadn't reached full strength after purging the poison, and the night's battle had left him physically and mentally exhausted. Nate's words just didn't make sense, no matter how much he concentrated.

"I'm lost," he admitted with a weary sigh.

"It was Lucas's idea." Shade's icy blue eyes watched him carefully. "The Council have been desperate to keep the rest of the Lore in the dark about the prophecy and Phoenix's existence. They'd shit kittens at the thought of humans finding out."

The mention of the mysterious blond vampire caused Phoenix to stiffen, and Ethan bit back the multitude of questions running through his head. It wasn't that he was complaining about the intervention, but Shade and Nate sure as hell had some explaining to do later.

Nate produced a small black mobile that looked suspiciously like an old flip phone. "We just need you to call your dad's cousin and specify our terms."

The phone was shoved into his hand, a number already on the screen, ready for him to dial. He looked up at Nate.

"Which are?"

In quick concise detail, it was all laid out. He chewed on the inside of his cheek as he listened and debated their options. Realistically, it wouldn't change anything in the long term; the prophecy still hung over their heads. But it would be nice not to have everyone trying to kill them while they figured it out. And they would figure it out. The alternative wasn't an option.

Unsurprisingly, William picked up on the first ring.

"What are you doing, Ethan?" The werewolf's familiar voice was tight with tension and an underlying warning; he wasn't alone.

"What we need to stay alive."

"You know the Council can't let you do this. The Mists will –"

"The Mists are no longer answering to the Council."

A long pause.

"If you expose her to the Lore, you'll just put her in more danger," William warned. "You know the Council won't be the only ones to believe her death is the answer."

Ethan barked out a laugh. "True. But we don't intend to just expose her to the Lore. We will be exposing the Lore to the humans. Then we'll all know what it's like to be in the firing line right alongside her."

He let the words, and their implications, sink in before continuing. "Our proposal is simple. The Council backs off and gives us time to stop the prophecy. I'm sure by now you've seen our I.T. capabilities. It will only take a push of a button for us to broadcast this internationally. And we *will* do it."

A low chuckle rumbled down the phone. "They're not going to like being given an ultimatum."

Ethan smiled. "Tough."

43

A bone-deep weariness settled over Phoenix, and she let the conversation drone on around her as she slouched over the kitchen island. The Council had kindly agreed to a temporary stay of execution, for which she was oh so honoured. They'd also received word from Cormac that all injuries were being tended to, himself included.

Two dead and a dozen severely injured. It was better than they could have hoped for, but it still felt like too high a price.

As it turned out, the vampires had been the only reason she and the others had made it to the community centre in the first place. The sudden disappearance of the Mists in the forest had not been down to their impressive show of power, but rather an unexpected attack from Lucas and his clan. It had done little more than delay the final showdown, but it had been enough to allow events to play out as they had.

She couldn't think too much about that though; her feelings for the blond vampire that sired her father were something she just didn't have the energy to examine at that moment.

When the front door opened an hour later, she jerked her head off the cool marble that had become her pillow. Her breath caught as Fia came into the kitchen, followed by Cormac, Sasha, and finally, Abi. A dizzying sense of relief overwhelmed her, and she leapt to her feet to pull her friend into a crushing embrace. Ethan had assured her that Abi was fine, but she couldn't help the sob that escaped her at seeing the evidence for herself. A part of her had truly believed she'd never see her friend again.

Teary laughter and slaps on the back all around proved she wasn't the only one feeling a little overwhelmed by their victory. Soon, they all retired to the cosy living room where a blazing fire provided hypnotic viewing, if not fully chasing away the pervasive chill. Fia busied herself making tea and laying out plates of meat and biscuits as everyone was brought up to speed.

"Eat up. You need to get your strength back." The order was directed at the entire room, but Fia's eyes fell on Phoenix and she gave a knowing smile.

As if by magic, Fia's words reminded her just how drained she was. Her limbs were leaden, and the warm spark that normally occupied the centre of her chest seemed weak and far away. The thought of sleeping for a week was more than appealing, and she snuggled back into the large cushions behind her on the sofa.

"You okay?" Ethan dropped down beside her, his brown eyes filled with concern.

"Long night, I guess." Hell, he didn't look so hot himself.

An odd feeling, almost like bubbles popping, drew her hand to her stomach, and she frowned.

"Let me get you something to eat," he offered.

She reached out a hand to stop him as he started to stand. "No, it's fine, I can –"

The room spun and her vision grew hazy. It lasted only a second and when everything came back into focus, she was aware of Ethan gripping her arm, a look of alarm on his face. Heat crept up her cheeks and she cringed. Maybe food wasn't such a bad idea; her blood sugar was obviously low.

Yet again showcasing a talent for mind reading, Fia appeared in front of her with a plate of food and a kind smile. "Here, this will help. It can take a lot out of you in the early stages."

Phoenix scrunched her brow in confusion, dimly wondering if her brain had short-circuited at some point during the night. "The early stages of what?"

Fia simply nodded her head towards the hand she had resting protectively on her stomach. Beside her, Ethan's jaw dropped, while she tried in vain to unravel what had to be the world's most confusing math equation.

"She's pregnant?" The question was barely a whisper from Ethan's mouth.

His mother nodded. "Only just, but the spark of life is strong."

Awe and anger and fear passed over his face all in the blink of an eye. "Why didn't you say anything?"

Fia's smile turned sad. "It only mattered if we survived. I couldn't take the chance that it would cloud your judgement in the fight."

Gripping terror clenched Phoenix's gut, and she wrapped her arms around her stomach. A child? How?

Of course, she knew how it physically happened; she could even now remember the feel of Ethan's body against hers as he held her close. But it didn't make sense. How could she have a baby? She'd barely survived the night, let alone the last couple of months. How could she be responsible for another living thing, never mind a defenceless baby?

Her legs were shaky under her as she stood up in a daze and muttered an excuse about needing to go to the bathroom – that was what pregnant women did, wasn't it?

She was vaguely aware of Ethan reaching out a hand towards her, and Fia quietly telling him to let her go. A sliver of guilt joined the fear twisting her gut, but she pushed it back and stumbled out of the room in need of air and a minute alone to think. She wandered aimlessly down the hall until she came to the staircase, then slumped down onto the bottom step.

"Phoenix?"

Abi's hesitant voice drew her attention from her knees to find worried blue eyes watching her. She opened her mouth to tell her friend everything was fine, then closed it again. When Abi motioned for her to scooch over on the stairs, she did, and they sat together in silence.

Eventually, she managed in a small voice, "I'm pregnant."

Abi's jaw dropped and her eyes widened in shock. Then her face morphed into a wide grin and she crouched down in front of Phoenix, taking both hands in hers.

"A baby?"

Phoenix nodded numbly. She'd been trying to make sense of the word ever since Fia's revelation. What did it even mean anyway? A baby. She had no context for it, no real life experience to equate it to, or no clue how she should be feeling.

"And you're not happy?" Abi asked, no judgement in her tone.

Tears pricked the back of her eyes and her stomach clenched. "How can I protect a baby, Abi? The Council won't let this go, no matter what they say. And then there's still the prophecy to deal with –"

"The prophecy." Abi jumped up suddenly, wringing her hands in excitement. "Oh my god, that's it! Don't you remember? It said, 'so long as she alone does stand.'"

Phoenix gawked at her friend, fully convinced she'd lost her mind.

Abi pulled her to her feet with a shake. "Don't you see? If you're having a baby, you won't be alone. You won't be the only hybrid."

44

When Phoenix finally got her head down, she slept for sixteen hours straight. She awoke feeling aches and pains in places she didn't even know she could hurt, with a nervous fluttering in her stomach that had nothing to do with the new life growing there.

After her talk with Abi, she'd pulled on her big girl pants and talked to Ethan. He'd agreed that Abi's theory had merit, and that thought alone had been the start of the tentative hope blossoming somewhere deep inside of her. But she kept that hope in check – they both did – with the unspoken understanding that they still had a long way to go if they were to have a chance of bringing their baby into this world.

Their baby. The words still didn't really make sense to her, not in any tangible form. She didn't dare let herself imagine either. And there would be no awkward "what are we to each other" conversations. Not yet. Not while the thread of hope was still so fragile.

It was with extreme effort that she pulled herself out of

bed and into the shower. After, she went in search of Lucas.

She'd slept long enough that night was once again shrouding them in darkness, and she had no problem finding him sitting at the island in the kitchen, nursing a warm cup of tea and some of Fia's homemade biscuits. She pulled out a stool beside him and sat down.

"I never thanked you. If it wasn't for you and your vampires, we may not have survived to be sitting here now."

The look he gave her was sombre. "It was the least I could do."

A heavy silence hung between them as they both acknowledged the history that caused them to be strangers to each other.

"Why did you come?"

Lucas sighed and looked at the mug of tea cupped in his hands. "Your father was like a brother to me. When he broke Council edict ... I couldn't risk bringing their wrath down on my clan. I was bound to protect them, but I couldn't kill him either. No matter what our laws say."

"So, you banished him."

"So, I banished him. Every instinct in me told me it was wrong, but it was too late. I had no idea where Marcus had gone. It was only when Shade contacted me that –"

"Shade?" She jerked her head up in surprise.

"He came to me requesting my help. Demanding it, actually. I didn't know about you, that Marcus and Aria had had a child. I didn't even think such a thing was possible. Shade told me about the prophecy and the Council's vendetta. He asked me if I was finally willing to do the right thing." Lucas looked at her, his grey eyes haunted. "I failed your father. I won't fail you."

She bit her lip and nodded before hopping down from the stool. His apology had come too late for the person it was intended for, and it reminded her that she had her own apology to make. She left him lost in his memories and went to find Shade.

A quick check with Nate sent her to the large garage adjoining the house. She found him there, viciously punishing a weathered punchbag. He stilled at her approach, but didn't turn to look at her.

"I owe you an apology." She pulled at the sleeve of her top, a childish voice in the back of her mind sulkily pointing out that he'd been a dick to her, so it wasn't surprising she'd suspected him.

He shrugged.

"Lucas said you sought him out. Why?"

The question finally caused him to turn. His expression was unreadable as he met her gaze with his icy blue eyes. "He loves you."

"Lucas?" She furrowed her brow in confusion.

His unreadable expression morphed into the irritated glare that was so much more familiar to her.

"Ethan. I don't want him to get hurt, so you need to stay alive." It was an order, not open to discussion or subject to emotion. He turned back to the punchbag, connecting with a solid left, right combo.

She stared at his back for a moment, confounded by the sullen vampire, but turned with a sigh to leave. His words stopped her in her tracks.

"The real fight is still to come, Phoenix. You'll need as many people on your side as possible if this world is to have a chance of surviving."

45

The vampire strained against his silver bonds. Foam dripped from his mouth as razor sharp fangs snapped at nothing. Crazed eyes turned fiery red and cast the metal walls of the sterile chamber in an eerie glow. A body lay slumped on the ground just out of reach, its lifeless eyes staring at the ceiling with a now permanent look of terror.

Darius walked a slow circle around their newest test subject, and a satisfied smile settled on his face as he stepped over the body without a glance. Everything was finally falling into place. Phoenix was alive, despite her continued stupidity, and for now, the Council posed no threat to his plans. It was time to take fate out of the equation.

His head of security stood quietly in front of the vampire, waiting for Darius to rejoin him before speaking.

"You were right," Erik confirmed. "We just needed to find the right kind of demon for the hosting to take. This one seems to be a good match for the vampire."

As Darius watched, shadows swirled behind the red fire

of the vampire's eyes and the snarling quietened. The straining stopped and the crazed look turned into something altogether more terrifying. The vampire tilted its head and regarded them with curiosity. Darius's smile widened.

"Let's test the other species to confirm their matches. Once we know the right combinations, we can move to the next phase."

The door to the chamber opened and Darius turned to the white-haired wolf who stood reluctantly in the doorway.

"Ah, Sean. How was your trip home? You weren't seen, I hope."

The Omega's jaw tightened, but he didn't answer. Instead, he averted his gaze to take in the chained vampire and lifeless body. His hand clenched around the door handle, and it snapped off with a crack.

Darius raised an eyebrow.

"I need you to bring me one of the wolves. I'll leave the choice up to you, though I suggest you choose one that's easy to control. They can become very unpredictable when the demon takes hold."

Not ready for it to end?

Well it doesn't have to because the Midnight Trilogy is now COMPLETE!

Continue the story in 1 Minute to Midnight

256

AUTHOR NOTE

Thank you for joining me on this new adventure through Ireland's hidden supernatural world. If you enjoyed this book, I would be very grateful if you could leave a brief review (it can be as short as you like) on the site where you purchased your copy.

As an author, reviews are the most powerful tools in my arsenal when it comes to getting attention for my books. Honest feedback goes a long way in increasing visibility and helping me to reach other readers like you, so thank you in advance!

*To get exclusive bonus material and be the first to hear about new releases, promotions, and giveaways **Sign up for my Newsletter at https://lmhatchell.com!***

A QUICK THANKS

You would think that after writing one book, it would get easier. But, nope. It was a big challenge to sit down and face that blank page again. So, I'm eternally grateful to the people that helped to bring this story to life.

For my guinea pig Sandra, who gets to read the worst version of my stories (or at least, the worst version that I let anyone see), and can still be guaranteed to be my best support. And for the Beta Bitch, who has been with me since book one but proved particularly invaluable for this story.

One of my favourite parts of the writing process is working through edits as the book reaches completion. It's at this point that I really start to fall in love with the story and see its potential come to life. I have my fantastic editors at Three Point Author Services to thank for that. With their feedback, I'm growing as a writer, and you get saved from some of my more annoying writing quirks 😉

Lastly, I owe a huge thanks to my partner and baby girl for keeping me on my toes and making sure I come back to the real world from time to time.